JOURNEY'S END

Guy said quietly, 'I was just wondering
. . . what you'd do if I kissed you.'

Cassie froze. In an instant, a confusion
of feelings tumbled into her mind, foremost of which was anger. She had been
right – all this had, after all, been a clever
way of getting her to relax with him, so
that he could make his move. And she
thought she knew, too, exactly why he
had decided to do it. He had met a girl
who did not fall at his feet within seconds,
and his pride couldn't take rejection . . .

He was still looking at her, waiting for
an answer to his question. Cassie took a
deep breath and replied levelly, 'I'd turn
around and walk out of this room.'

'Why?'

He had moved closer to her, and the
dark-fringed grey eyes were alight. Suddenly something inside Cassie snapped . . .

Journeys end in lovers meeting
                    — **Twelfth Night**

JOURNEY'S END

ANNA STANTON

A Sapphire Romance

JOURNEY'S END
ISBN 0 600 20068X

First published in Great Britain 1981
by Hamlyn Paperbacks

Printed and marketed by
RCA Direct Marketing, 1133 Avenue of the Americas
New York, N. Y. 10036

Printed in the U. S. A.

1

Alan Blythe emerged from the aircraft and paused at the top of the steps to squint up at the leaden and extremely wet sky. With a wry grin he said to the girl at his side, 'Welcome to England!'

The downpour had turned Heathrow into a dismal grey waste; sodden concrete, streaming glass and a vast dull smear of water on the tarmac. Cassie MacRae suppressed a shiver as she took it all in and hitched her lightweight cream jacket more closely round her shoulders, wishing she'd worn something warmer. The rain stung her face like needles as she and Alan made their way down the steps with the other passengers from the Qantas flight, and she thought ruefully of her light shoes, which wouldn't do much to keep her feet dry. It was only a short walk to the terminal, but she guessed that by the time they reached the shelter of the building she'd be as near wet through as made no difference. It certainly was a bit of a culture-shock—not two days ago she had been basking in the hot Sydney sun, and now this. England. *Yech*.

'Lovely, isn't it?' Alan said cheerfully. 'Does wonders for your tan!'

'Is it always like this?' Cassie had to shout to be heard over the whining jet-scream of a Boeing that had started taxiing from its berth towards the runway.

Alan laughed. 'Of course—the British are born with gills instead of lungs, didn't you know?' They ducked at last into the shelter of the noisy terminal and he reached out to tweak a length of blonde hair that fell, now rather damply, over her shoulders. 'And I did warn you about the English spring.'

'Too right you did, but I should have listened harder. It's so *cold!*'

They had joined the queue that was straggling slowly towards Customs. In the background a loudspeaker blared, announcing the departure of a Miami flight, and she added, listening, 'It's a pity they couldn't have shot this film in Florida. It would have been a bit more like home!'

'Don't worry, Cass. In an hour or so we'll be snug in the bar of one of the best hotels in London. It'll all look different then. And once we get going, if I have anything to do with it, you'll be too busy to worry about the weather.'

Alan was nothing if not an optimist, Cassie thought; it was impossible to stay down for too long in his company. She gave in, and grinned. 'Okay, boss!'

'That's better. And boss knows best, right?'

'Right. Have you got your passport?'

He fumbled in his jacket pocket. 'Somewhere, I think . . . Oh hell, where did I put it?'

'Try your flight bag.' She pointed at a tell-tale corner sticking out of the bag's side pocket, and as he fished the passport out Alan said, 'All right, I know—where would I be without you? Hey, that looks like our luggage coming out of that chute over there—'

Twenty minutes later they were through Customs and Immigration, and making their way towards the outside of the terminal. At the glass doors a middle-aged man in a chauffeur's uniform stepped out of nowhere. 'Mr. Blythe?'

'That's right.'

'There's a car waiting for you, sir, from Mr. Hamer. If you'd like to come this way.' He took two of the cases, and Alan and Cassie exchanged a raised eyebrow as they followed him.

'VIP treatment,' Cassie observed with a grin. 'They must think you're someone important.'

He swiped playfully at her. 'Cheeky woman! Any more of that and you'll be on the next flight back to Sydney.'

They walked out into the rain again and Cassie privately thought that that wouldn't have been such a bad idea. But as the chauffeur held open the door of a sleek black Daimler and she settled herself comfortably in the plush leather seat some of her misgivings began to fade. After all, this was an adventure, and not many girls of twenty-two would ever have the chance of working on such an exciting project. Maybe England wasn't going to be so bad.

If Heathrow had been a disappointment, the Albury Hotel was anything but. A stone's throw from Park Lane, it towered elegantly skywards, dominating the older and smaller buildings around it. Alan and Cassie were disgorged from their car, which purred off into the afternoon traffic, and walked into a vast lobby that dazzled the eye with its sheer elegance. Thick carpet muted the footfalls of the well-dressed guests who drifted through, and the mirrored ceiling was supported by slim pillars finished in onyx. As soon as the receptionist learned Alan's name the service became almost embarrassing; they were whisked in an express lift to the ninth floor and shown down a broad corridor to the rooms that were to be home for the next few weeks.

Alan had been given a suite to himself, which was fair enough, and Cassie found herself in a room three doors away. Not wanting to give the porter the impression that she didn't do this kind of thing every day, she suppressed a gasp of sheer astonished delight when the door opened, and managed to keep her wits enough to give him a generous tip before he left. But as soon as the door closed she let out her breath loudly. VIP treatment indeed, she thought. The room was very large and decorated in several shades of brown, ranging from the mushroom-coloured hessian on the walls through warm cinnamon curtains and bed-spread to a dark chocolate carpet that was so luxurious it made her want to lie down and roll over and over like a self-indulgent cat. There were a couple of prints on the walls, and the wide picture window gave a view over London that was a photographer's dream. A wardrobe and a well-lit vanity unit had been built into one wall, and when she explored further she found an adjoining bathroom with a mushroom-coloured suite and towels that precisely matched the shade of the carpet.

Cassie looked down at her own damp clothes and at the travel-worn cases with their dozens of peeling stickers, and felt horribly out of place. Best to get these unpacked and stowed away as fast as possible; they looked too seedy to lie around in such an opulent room. And she'd have a shower, change and—

A tap on the door stopped her in mid-thought and Alan came in.

'Well? What do you think?'

'It's fantastic!' She kicked off her? shoes. 'What's yours like?'

8

'Oh, it makes this one look like a pigsty! How's the bed?'

'You've got a one-track mind,' she rebuked as he crossed the room and bounced on the double divan.

'I know, and a lot of good it does me! I've been lusting passionately after you for years, Cassie MacRae, but will you give me a chance?' Clowning, he made a mock-sad face and dropped to his knees on the floor, clasping both hands to his heart. Cassie laughed.

'Shut up, Alan! Stop playing the fool will you?' That was one of the things she liked most about working with him. You could always count on Alan to be a joker, and, as with most things, he didn't give up easily. Now he was knee-walking towards her and acting like a Shakespearean ham. 'Ah, Cassie, Cassie!' He made a grab for her leg and she skipped out of range.

'Idiot! We're here on business, remember?'

'Okay.' He raised his hands in defeat and stood up, but couldn't resist a parting shot. 'In a couple of days I'll be surrounded by beautiful little dollies all craving my body, and then you'll be sorry!'

He was probably right, she thought—at least about the first part. Alan collected lovely girls wherever he went, and although his job had a lot to do with it, there was no denying that he was a very attractive man. There was something little-boyish about his cheerful and fresh-complexioned face, and when he felt like turning on the charm his brown eyes could twinkle in a way guaranteed to produce instant results. If it hadn't been for their business relationship Cassie knew she could have fallen for him herself, but as it was she was so used to him, had become such a good friend to him, that the idea was ludicrous; he was almost like a brother to her.

From being the court jester Alan suddenly switched back to a more serious and businesslike mood. Brushing at his trousers he said, 'What I really came in for was to tell you that Van Hamer's just telephoned me. He wants to meet us for a drink in the bar at six, before we all have dinner together.'

'He moves fast.'

'Yeah, so I gather from what I've already seen of him. Thing is, love, I need to build up on the good impression I made when I saw him in Australia—he's the moneybags behind this film, and we've got to keep him sweet. So if you could dress up to kill, flutter your eyelashes a bit and still show that you know what you're talking about...'

She nodded. 'Generally be the perfect personal assistant with a bit of glamour attached?'

Alan looked apologetic. 'Exactly. Now, you've not met him before, but take it from me, he's an almighty creep. But contract or no contract, he's powerful enough to make life awkward if he changes his mind about liking me.'

'He won't,' she told him with a sudden smile. Although he didn't normally show it, she could tell that Alan wasn't as confident as he appeared, and she wanted to reassure him that she, at least, had total faith in him. He wasn't much taller than she was, and she leaned forward to plant a sisterly kiss on his nose. 'He likes you because you're the best in the business. Just you remember that!'

Alan's eyes warmed and he hugged her. 'Thanks, Cass. I'll see you in the Terrace Bar at six, okay?'

'Fine.' She watched him go, then set about the task of unpacking her cases. She'd probably brought far too many clothes, but in this kind of life you could never tell what might be needed. Now—it was four-thirty (she'd set her watch by British time as the plane came in to land): that gave her an hour and a half. Time for a shower, and then maybe she could put her feet up for a few minutes before the first ordeal began.

By a quarter to six Cassie was ready. She had discovered a colour TV set in a wall cabinet, and while she applied the finishing touches to her makeup she listened to the early evening news, but her mind wasn't on the reader's voice. She was feeling nervous and wondering how this first meeting with Van Hamer was going to turn out.

The plain fact was that this was the biggest break Alan had ever had since he had started out on the highly perilous road of an up-and-coming young film director. It was a road that she was convinced would take him to the top, if there was any justice in the world. He'd made four films in Australia, two under the auspices of the influential National Film Board, and was already winning the kind of critical acclaim that was the envy of a lot of men with twice his experience. Alan was one of the new breed of forward-thinking and imaginative film men who were starting to give Hollywood a run for its money, and it was that quality which had attracted the interest of Van Hamer.

Van Hamer was big news. His reputation was formidable and his photograph had been plastered all over almost every trade magazine for the best part of a decade. He owned or co-owned (she wasn't quite sure) an influential and prosperous production company, and any project to which his name was attached was a sure-fire success. Six months ago he had started scouting around for young talent, and in particular a director who was climbing the rungs of the success ladder but still malleable enough to be moulded to fit into the Van Hamer stable. He had heard of Alan, seen his films, liked them and arrived in Sydney to view the young Australian for himself. After a few meetings and discussions, the offer had been made for Alan to direct a new film in London.

Cassie still remembered the yell of delight Alan had let out when Van Hamer's official letter arrived after his return to England—the whole office had reverberated with it. And from then on his life and hers had become a mad whirl of meetings, script readings and casting, until almost before she knew what had happened she was boarding the flight for London.

And now, this was it. She was to come face to face with the Big Man for the first time. All very well for Alan; he knew what to expect, how to handle Hamer. But she didn't want to put a single foot wrong, and the idea of being put in the spotlight, so to speak, before the one man on whom Alan's reputation probably depended was nerve-racking. If this film took off, he was made. If it didn't, he could wave goodbye to his career. And that, she was fully aware, was the one thing that could break his heart.

The TV newscast was beginning to irritate her. She switched the set off and then opened the wardrobe door to take a look at herself in the full-length mirror. She had chosen a slim-fitting black knee-length dress with shoulder straps, over which she wore a matching black jacket. It gave an intriguing impression that was half-way between the severe and the provocative, and she'd wondered at first if she was overdoing it. On the other hand, it was probably best to hit Van Hamer between the eyes from the start. Alan, she was sure, would approve. And anyway, it set off a suntan that would be the envy of most English people at this time of year. She'd left her hair loose, only looping back twin strands from the front and catching them at the back of her head, and she thought as she gazed at the mirror that she looked more than passable. She had lost half a stone through dieting in the summer and her figure was as slim and leggy as anyone could have wished. She ignored, as she always did, the little voice inside her that told her her nose was too pert, and her green eyes laughed back at her from the glass as she struck a pose. Just about ready—all she needed now was a whiff of perfume, and a notebook and pen to add weight to the Efficient Secretary side of the image.

She sprayed herself liberally with an Yves Saint-Laurent cologne that Alan had given her for Christmas and left the room to make her way down to the bar. In the corridor two well-dressed men ogled her openly and she felt glad of the little ego-boost, aware that there were butterflies in her stomach. The lift swept her down to the first floor, and as she stepped out of it she touched wood for luck.

It was two minutes past six when Cassie walked into the Terrace Bar. The bar was as opulent as the rest of the hotel, decorated in soft greens and served by a swarm of waiters who scurried between the tables like ants. As she entered, one of the ants glided towards her and asked if he could help madame.

Cassie glanced around. 'I'm looking for Mr. Alan Blythe and Mr. Van Hamer.'

'Certainly, madame—they have a table by the window. If madame will follow me...' He led the way between seated groups of wealthy-looking drinkers, through waves of heady perfume that made Cassie wonder if perhaps she should have emptied the Saint-Laurent bottle over her head and been done with it.

Alan and Van Hamer were sitting at the far side of

13

the bar on a raised marble terrace flanked by an amber glass wall that looked over the Mayfair rush hour. Alan, too, had dressed for the occasion in an off-white safari suit, and Cassie felt almost possessively proud of him. He looked poised, confident and cool, with no trace of the nerves he must be suffering, and when he saw her he rose.

'Cassie! Come and sit down—meet Van Hamer. Mr. Hamer, this is my personal assistant, Cassie MacRae.'

Van Hamer rose and extended a hand, looking hard at her. He was a small man, smaller than Alan, and lightly built. His complexion was pale but his hair, cut short and receding, was dark, almost black. A small beard fringed his narrow but strong jaw, and his eyes and mouth were small. He looked like a not very attractive elf, and it occurred to her, flippantly, that he would have made a good movie vampire.

'Miss MacRae.' There was an accent; it sounded like a cross between Dutch and New York. 'A pleasure. Please sit down and join us in a glass of champagne. We're here to celebrate, after all.' He poured her a glass, then raised his own. 'To our mutual success, Alan.'

Alan smiled, and they all drank.

'Now.' Van Hamer smoothed a folder that lay on the table before him. 'As I've been saying, there's not really much more to clear up. We begin filming on Monday, which gives you five days to get acquainted with everyone on the set. The scriptwriter's arriving tomorrow—he should have been here earlier, but he got held up in Madrid—and there's a conference suite at this hotel which I've booked for our use. You shouldn't come across any problems, but if you do, just let me know. I'm at my Soho office most days—

you've got the number, so all your secretary needs to do is call me.' He glanced at Cassie, who felt stung by the remark. She would have liked to point out that she wasn't Alan's secretary, but his personal assistant, and suddenly she wished that she hadn't dressed up, despite what Alan had said. Van Hamer had probably passed her off as just another bird-brain with visions of breaking into stardom. There'd be time enough to put him right on that later.

'In the meantime,' Hamer was saying, 'I've arranged a small meeting for eight-thirty tonight between the key people on the film. Our star performers' (Cassie thought he said the word 'performers' with a hint of a sneer) 'will be there, and if there are any disagreements about the script we can try and iron them out on the spot, to save time later. It's a pity about the damned scriptwriter of course, but if he's stuck in Madrid he's stuck in Madrid. Anyway, we don't need his approval for any changes. On what he's earning, he's not in a position to complain.'

Judging by the look that crossed Alan's face briefly, Cassie guessed that his opinion of Van Hamer was on a par with her own. He struck her as a man who treated his subordinates as a Victorian aristocrat might treat household servants, and the way he had dismissed the scriptwriter's importance confirmed it. The chances were that Alan would come in for much the same treatment before long. Still, Hamer wasn't the only fish in the sea. With luck, Alan could make use of what he had to offer, build up his own reputation, then move on before the company really got its claws into him. But in the meantime he would have to swallow his pride and put up with it.

A waiter materialised by Van Hamer's shoulder.

'Mr. Hamer—your table is ready.'

Hamer nodded and waved the man away. 'All right, Alan. We'll talk technicalities tonight with the others. Until then, I suggest we relax over dinner.' He rose. 'The chef here's not a genius, but he is passable.'

He left the table without waiting for them, and Alan raised his eyebrow as he ushered Cassie before him. 'Real charmer, isn't he?' he whispered in her ear.

'Secretary, indeed!' she hissed back, still smarting. 'Is he paying for this meal?'

'He'd better be!'

'Then I'm going to eat like a pig.'

2

As she and Alan returned to their rooms after the meal, Cassie began to feel her first symptoms of jet-lag. Stepping out of the lift she yawned suddenly, feeling a vast wave of tiredness wash over her. Alan gave her a sympathetic glance. 'Is all that flying starting to catch up with you?'

'Yes...' she stifled another yawn. 'I suppose I should be used to it by now, but that was one hell of a long haul. Providing I can get a good night's sleep and don't have to get up early, I should be all right tomorrow though.'

Alan nodded. 'I could do with a decent kip myself. What about the meeting tonight? You can cry off if you want to.'

It was very tempting, but Cassie shook her head. After all, she was here to do a job and she didn't want to let Alan down. 'No. You'll need me to take notes. Maybe I can put my head down for half an hour before the meeting starts.'

Alan grinned. She opened the door to her room and he followed her in. 'You can't fool me! You just want to get a look at the stars of the show and see how they match up to our home-grown Aussie talent.'

She pulled a face at him and flopped down on to the bed. 'I couldn't care less about them. Providing they don't give you any trouble when you're working, I'm not interested.'

'Nuts! You're dying to get your sticky paws on the irresistible Guy Carver, and don't try and deny it. You women are all the same!'

'Oh yes, I've read all about *him,*' Cassie said darkly. 'God's gift to women and the acting world at large. That I could do without, thanks very much.'

She remembered that Alan had been both pleased and apprehensive when Guy Carver had finally been contracted to take the lead role in the film. Certainly he was a box-office crowd-puller—in the last five years he had become one of the top stars on the British market, and also one of the few big names who hadn't deserted for America, but his personal reputation was something else again. Hardly a week went by without his name appearing in a gossip column; he seemed to spend his entire life in an endless round of parties and jet-set social occasions, where he usually managed to be at the centre of any scandal that was going on. He was permanently surrounded by beautiful girls, whose hearts he broke as casually as anyone might break a piece of bread.

More than one starlet whose dreams of reforming him had been shattered had confessed the 'intimate details' to a Sunday paper, and Guy Carver emerged from those reports as cold, egotistical and altogether unpleasant. At least, that was what Cassie had firmly decided after reading all she could about Alan's leading actor in preparation for the film. She couldn't deny that he was extremely good-looking, but she was well prepared to dislike him from the start, on principle. Believing that forewarned is forearmed, she had already decided what her attitude to him was to be— cool, businesslike and otherwise utterly disinterested.

If Guy Carver thought she was going to be just another dolly-bird who would flutter her eyelashes and sigh at him, he had another think coming.

'Spare a thought for me,' Alan said plaintively, 'I got to direct him! Still, I've got to admit he's good. The whole damn' cast's good, if it comes to that. Janey Moore, Anna Loriot—'

'Anna Loriot. She *does* intrigue me,' Cassie interrupted. Madame Loriot was French, an ageing but still influential actress who had lived in retirement in Paris for seven years. 'How on earth did the company persuade her to come out of hiding? I thought she'd sworn never to appear on the screen again. Remember that interview in—'

'Oh, *that*. Some journalists wouldn't know the difference between a true story and the back view of a wallaby! A woman like Anna Loriot can't stay away from the world for too long. Besides, you just try keeping up her kind of lifestyle on back royalties!'

'You think it was money, then?'

'Well, I know that Hamer offered her a very fat deal indeed. But it's not just that. She's a professional; she wanted to work again and she liked the idea of this part.' Alan shrugged. 'Which suits me fine.'

Cassie frowned, trying to visualise Anna Loriot in the role written for her. In one sense it was rather close to reality; she would play a wealthy ex-singer and society darling now on the downward slope towards obscurity, but still with plenty to offer. In the film she was to fall in love with a young man struggling for fame (played, of course, by Carver) and Janey Moore would be her penniless rival with nothing to give but herself. Of course, as it was a 'weepy', young love triumphed in the end, but though it was not the most original of ideas, it would go down well at the cinemas. Also, the quality of the cast—and, as Cassie kept telling Alan firmly, the director—was enough to lift it out of the ordinary and make it a money-spinner. And Anna Loriot's role was a very sympathetic one, which she would fit into well...

Suddenly Alan snapped his fingers in front of Cassie's face. 'Hey, dreamy! Are you going to sleep on me?'

'No, sorry, I was miles away. What's the time?'

'Quarter to eight.'

She grimaced. 'That gives me about half an hour to have a rest.'

'Okay, I get the hint. The meeting's in Hamer's suite at eight-thirty. I'll see you there, all right?' He headed for the door. 'Sweet dreams!'

When Alan had gone, Cassie lay down on the bed, having first asked room service to call her in half an hour. Her mind was whirling with the events of the day, and when she closed her eyes she could see nothing but the image of the back of an aircraft seat. Her sense of time was completely upset, and it felt more like three a.m. than early evening. All she wanted was to sleep. But instead she had to get herself ready and appear bright and fresh and on the ball for a meeting with a blasted film producer and a bunch of blasted actors.

God almighty, MacRae, what are you complaining about? she asked herself. Here she was, moaning because she had a job that just about every other girl in the world would give her right arm for. Mixing with the stars, going on location, travelling all over the globe—it was the next best thing to being a celebrity herself! But right at this moment, she thought, she would have cheerfully exchanged it all for the chance to be in her own bed back home in Australia.

Never mind; it would all look different in the morning. Or it had better. With another wide yawn she closed her eyes, and was asleep within two minutes.

Van Hamer's suite was on the hotel's eighth floor. It seemed, in fact, that his company had virtually taken over three entire floors of the building for the duration of the filming. While a large number of the cast and crew lived in London—or close enough to make no difference—plenty didn't, and no expense had been spared to ensure that everyone was put up comfortably. It didn't seem in keeping with Hamer's character, and Cassie privately felt that it must be a tax loss.

She found when she walked into the suite at eight-thirty that no expense had been spared here either. To one side of the reception room stood a table almost collapsing under the weight of bottles and glasses, and not only a hotel staff barman but also a waiter were in attendance. Ten or twelve people stood around chatting idly, and Cassie saw that Alan had arrived before her. Signalling to catch his eye, she went to join him.

And then she saw whom he was talking to.

The man had his back to Cassie, but as she approached he turned round and fixed her with frank, assessing grey eyes fringed with startlingly black lashes. His hair too was black, curling on the nape of his neck and moulding a bonily handsome face with a long, straight nose and arrogant mouth. He was quite tall, but not so tall that she had to crane her neck to look at him, and was dressed impeccably yet casually in a military blue shirt and jeans that looked as though they had been tailored for him.

'Well, Alan, so this is your assistant,' said Guy Carver.

Cassie blinked, somewhat taken aback. On first impression, she decided that none of Guy Carver's photographs had ever done him justice. With all her prejudices in mind, even she had to admit that he was not much short of devastating. But that didn't mean she had to like him, and already there was something about his voice—a hint of condescension, the way he'd talked about her as if she wasn't there—that made her hackles rise.

Alan, maybe sensing that the actor's tone had already annoyed her, said hastily, 'Yes—Cassie, meet our star, Guy Carver. Guy, this is Cassie MacRae.'

'Cassie MacRae.' He let the name slip from his tongue elegantly. 'Alan has very good taste. Is Cassie short for Cassandra?'

He had a beautiful voice all right, cultured and modulated; but it didn't impress her in the least. 'No,' she said frostily, 'it's short for Cassie.'

Guy raised his eyebrows. 'Very pretty. And you're here to make sure everything runs smoothly?'

'I'm here to help Alan,' she said, thinking, *patronizing pig!* 'That's what I'm paid for.'

He ignored the barb. 'From what I've heard, he's the one who's going to be doing most of the helping. As I was saying before you arrived, Cassie, I saw one of Alan's films in Cannes two years ago. He's a real professional. It's a pity there aren't a few more around like him.' He smiled at Alan, and Cassie was surprised by the sincerity in his voice. Whatever else he might be, Guy Carver didn't shrink from giving praise where praise was due. Maybe, she thought, he was only intolerable with women, or in his private life. If that

22

was the case, she'd have to make sure he knew which side of the fence she was on.

Guy turned to her again. 'Alan tells me you've been with him for some time now.'

'Three years.'

'Any ambitions to become a director yourself? There seem to be quite a lot of women going in for it these days.'

'I haven't got the talent,' she told him, 'and I don't mind admitting it.'

He laughed. 'Rare honesty! And you don't want to be a film star, either?'

'No thanks. I've seen what they have to go through—I'm too lazy.'

'You mean you couldn't stand the pace of having hordes of gigolos fawning at your feet?'

Their eyes met, and Cassie hesitated, not sure whether or not he was laughing at her. 'Something like that,' she said.

'Well spoken.' Guy laid a hand on her shoulder, which she resented. 'Mind you, with a face and figure like yours I doubt if you'd have much difficulty, if you ever changed your mind.'

It was a shallow, suave remark, and struck Cassie more like an insult than a compliment. Obviously he had already assessed her and decided she was another typical hanger-on who would fall for that sort of mean-ingless flattery. She side-stepped so that his hand slipped from her shoulder, and gave him a cool smile but said nothing.

Van Hamer rescued them at that moment by ap-pearing in their midst. 'Alan—Cassie.' He nodded to them. 'Sorry about this delay—we're waiting for Anna, as usual. I suppose when you get to her age you can claim some privileges, but she never could read a watch. Have you all got a drink?'

Cassie said she hadn't, and Guy spoke up. 'I'll get you one. They do a good marguerita here—I imagine that's your kind of drink.'

It was, but wild horses wouldn't have made Cassie say so. 'I'd rather have a vodka and orange, thanks,' she said as he led her towards the table.

'Really? How sophisticated.' The sarcasm was unmistakable; he knew she was deliberately being awkward, and was retaliating. As he ordered the drink, and scotch with ice for himself, Cassie thought, *Mustn't overdo it, or he'll think I'm behaving like this to hide some kind of burning passion!*

'Thank you,' she said more pleasantly as he handed her a glass.

'My pleasure. Now, what shall we drink to?'

'I think the success of the film might be a good idea. If it fails, we'll all be the worse off.'

'To the film, then.' They drank, and he added, looking at her searchingly, 'Do you think it will be a failure?'

'No, I don't!'

'You're very loyal to Alan, aren't you?'

He might have expected Cassie to bridle at that, but she didn't. 'Yes, I am,' she told him honestly. 'He's great to work for, and I think he's got a lot of talent.'

There was an edge to her voice, and immediately Guy raised a hand in a defensive gesture. 'Don't get me wrong, I wasn't implying that he hasn't. Personally, I think Alan's a very fine director, and I'm looking forward to working with him. There, that's the truth—does it make you feel better?'

He was smiling at her impishly, and despite her

resentment she had to laugh. 'I'm sorry, Mr. Carver—'

'Guy.'

'Guy. I'm not at my best right now; I need a good night's sleep.'

'First time in England?'

'Yes.'

'You'll love it, when it stops raining. That's why I've always resisted the temptation of moving over to Hollywood, and why I've never become a tax exile. You get used to a place, grow to love it, put down roots—well, roots of a kind, anyway. Not that I haven't had the chance of course, but . . .' he hesitated. 'I'm an incurable Englishman. Finish your drink and let me get you another.'

Cassie looked down at her glass. 'No, thanks. I'm supposed to be working this evening.'

'Please yourself.' Suddenly his attitude had changed subtly; he was almost dismissive. Turning to the barman, he ordered another whisky. The silence between them became uncomfortable, and Cassie searched her mind for some small-talk to break it. At last she said, 'Where *do* you live?'

Guy's mouth twitched in a smile that didn't have much humour. 'Oh, that's what they all want to know. I keep it a closely guarded secret.'

She felt herself redden. As if she would want to know so that she could turn up uninvited on his doorstep one night . . . but that was probably what he was used to.

Guy sipped at his fresh drink, watching her, and she wasn't sure that she liked the look; it was cynical and amused, as if he was having some private joke at her expense. But before either of them could speak again there was a commotion on the other side of the room and, turning, Cassie saw that Anna Loriot had arrived.

She was a tiny woman, but her presence had an immediate effect. People hurried to greet her, and as she peered into the group Cassie saw Van Hamer—the cold fish Van Hamer—actually kiss her hand.

Beside her, Guy laughed, but there was affection in the sound. 'There she is at last, the old tyrant!'

'Is she?' Cassie knew that Mme. Loriot was noted for being difficult.

'Some people think so,' Guy said. 'I'll leave you to judge for yourself. Do you want to meet her?'

One difficult film star a day was enough for Cassie, but—'I suppose I ought to,' she said.

'Come on. I'll introduce you.' He led her towards the group standing around Anna, elbowed his way between Van Hamer's press secretary and the first assistant director, and said, 'Anna! How are you?'

She looked round, then saw him. 'Guy! *Chéri, comment ça va?*' And she planted a smacking kiss on his cheek as he stooped over her. They exchanged a stream of voluble French which Cassie didn't understand, then Guy swung round and drew her forward.

'Anna, meet Cassie MacRae. She's Alan Blythe's personal assistant, so if anything goes wrong she's the girl to scream at.'

At close quarters Anna Loriot was like a tiny, fragile bird. She must have been seventy, but her skin, though wrinkled, was fresh and without a blemish. She wore black with a triple rope of pearls at her slim throat, and her rich brown hair, now greying, was looped up in a soft style. Her huge brown eyes were wise and humorous and shrewd. She reminded Cassie

26

a little of Edith Piaf, and she had something of the same mysterious sadness.

'*Enchantée*, my dear.'

'Madame Loriot—it's a pleasure to meet you.' A corny greeting, but Cassie didn't know what else to say.

Mme. Loriot smiled brilliantly, showing perfect teeth. 'Ah! You too are Australian. How do you like England?'

'It's a little cold for me,' Cassie admitted.

'Cold? You understate, my dear! England is a miserable, wet place, and London is the worst part of it—so vulgar. Englishmen like Guy are notoriously fond of their wretched country, and it does them good to hear us foreigners tell the truth about it once in a while. Remember that, yes?'

Cassie returned the old woman's smile, feeling suddenly warm inside. 'I will, madame.'

'Good! Now, where is Alan? And where has Van disappeared to? I thought we were to have an important meeting here tonight?' She swept through the throng and headed towards the bar, calling out to Van Hamer, who was ordering her a drink. 'Van, do you intend to stand there forever mixing cocktails? We are here to work, *n'est-ce pas?*'

Guy laughed, and Cassie saw Alan sidling up to her. 'Magnificent, isn't she?' he whispered in her ear.

She turned. 'Incredible! She'll have us all on our toes.'

'Yes—and that's where you're going to come in handy.'

'What do you mean?'

'Well...' Alan looked sheepish, and she knew something was coming that she wouldn't like. 'It's like this, Cass. You're going to have a fair bit of time on your hands while we're actually filming, so I thought maybe, well, maybe you could do your bit towards keeping the stars happy.'

Cassie looked blankly at him. 'Like what, Alan?'

'We-ell, seeing that they're comfortable, getting drinks, doing a bit of chauffeuring, booking restaurants, whatever. It won't amount to much, but—' he grinned boyishly, like a dog trying to wheedle its way into someone's good books. It was his favourite ploy, and she always fell for it. She gave a snort of laughter.

'You mean be a general dogsbody? Oh, *Alan!*'

'Come on, Cass. A big favour for boss-man. If I have to put up with that temperamental pair off-set as well as on, I'll be a nervous wreck within a week. All I really want is for you to keep them out of my hair.'

She held up her hands in defeat. 'Okay. Since you put it like that, and you're paying my wages, I can't refuse, can I, boss-man?'

Alan hugged her. 'I knew you'd see it my way— good girl! Now, got your notebook and pencil ready?'

Making a mock-martyred face, Cassie held them up.

'Right. As they say, let's get this show on the road!'

The meeting lasted something over an hour, during which Cassie took what minutes she could pick out from the hubbub of talk. It seemed there were still a few matters to be sorted out before filming began. The location scenes were to be done in London, and once they were completed the whole crew would shift to a studio for the indoor work. The schedule was very tight, but everyone had resigned themselves to the fact that they were in for an exhausting period.

On the whole, Cassie decided, with one or two exceptions the cast and crew were a likeable crowd. She had been introduced to a few more key people, including Janey Moore, the actress playing the younger female lead, and had liked her immediately. She was a quiet, unassuming girl with enough experience to fulfil Alan's prayer for real professionals to work with, and she was also happily married, which meant there would be no off-set tantrums with Guy Carver. Then there was Peter Gates, the insipid-looking but determined assistant director, and Andrew Symes.

Cassie wasn't really sure why Andrew Symes was at the meeting at all. Tall, big-built and sandy-haired, he was Guy Carver's agent, and Cassie didn't see why, with the contract signed, sealed and delivered, he might be needed. He and Guy hardly spoke to each other throughout the evening. Yet he seemed very friendly with Van Hamer, so she supposed it was something to do with the old-boy network, and that Symes was along for the ride.

The formalities broke up shortly before eleven, and Hamer insisted that everyone stay for a drink before they went their separate ways. It wasn't long before Cassie found herself face to face with Guy once more. He sauntered up to where she was standing by the window looking out at the seemingly endless spread of twinkling lights, and said, 'How's the perfect secretary?'

Cassie looked up. 'Perfect, thanks. Are you happy with the meeting?'

'Yes, I think so.' He paused. 'And what are you going to do now?'

'Go to my room, lock the door and go to bed with the phone off the hook. And sleep.'

Guy smiled amusedly. 'What a waste. I thought perfect secretaries didn't need to bother with little things like sleep.'

There was a bantering tone to his voice that she didn't like, and she retorted, 'No. Unlike actors, we're only human.'

Guy's eyes became colder. 'In which case I'll take the hint and leave you to your solitary bed. It's been a pleasure talking to you.' There was sarcasm in the last sentence, and Cassie felt her blood boiling as she watched him walk away. She was still staring after him when a voice at her side said, 'Don't tell me you have already had a brush with our leading man?'

Anna Loriot stood a few feet away, her eyes twinkling mischievously.

'Oh—not really, madame.' Cassie smiled. 'But I think he was expecting me to fall for his charm, and he was surprised when I didn't.'

The Frenchwoman laughed throatily. 'Oh, take no notice. He is used to the more—what is the word— *pretentious* kind of ladies who hover on the fringe of his world. Now he finds a girl who is different, who is honest, and he does not know how to react.'

'Thank you for the compliment.' Suddenly Cassie felt a glow of pleasure. 'I don't deserve it.'

'Nonsense! I have been watching you, *chérie,* and I have seen. You do not dress up like a bird of paradise, you do not flutter the eyelashes at handsome or important men. Like us, you are here to work, and that makes you one of us, you see?' Before Cassie could reply the old woman tapped her firmly on the arm with one finger. 'But you should not take too much notice of Guy. He loves women, and yet he does not *like* them, if you understand me. But his bark is worse than his bite.'

Cassie thought privately that that was probably the best description of Guy Carver's character she had yet heard. 'I'll remember that, madame,' she promised.

Her companion pursed her mouth in annoyance. 'Anna, my dear, call me Anna! We are friends, yes? Friends do not call each other *madame*. So, now you have a drink with me and tell me all about Australia.'

It would have been impossible to refuse, though what Cassie really wanted was to fall into bed and sleep for at least twelve hours. She followed Anna towards the bar and listened as she ordered the barman to make up two highly complicated cocktails. As the frustrated man did his best Anna turned and whispered in Cassie's ear.

'You see, I have the reputation of a tyrant! But it is all sham; I am not really anything of the kind. But I am small, and small people have to fight harder to be noticed. So I bark and I snap, and they jump!' She took the two glasses, handed one to Cassie, '*A votre santé!* If you do not sleep after this, I shall despair of you!'

Cassie laughed, caught up in Anna's good humour. As she drank, she felt grateful that she had already made one friend.

3

On the Saturday before filming started, Van Hamer threw a party.

It took place in the hotel, and was like no party Cassie had ever seen in her life. The general idea was to wish the film *bon voyage,* and just about everyone who could possibly have anything to do with it was there. At nine p.m. Cassie walked into the Charles II suite—all the hotel's conference and party rooms were named after English monarchs—and stopped.

'Good grief,' she said in an undertone to Alan, who stood beside her. 'I knew Van Hamer had money, but this is ridiculous!'

The room was jam-packed with people, all of whom seemed to be trying to outdo each other in appearance. It looked as though all the women had spent the whole day scouring London's most exclusive shops to find the trendiest clothes in town, and, looking down at her own long Grecian-style dress in clingy silver-grey silk, she felt suddenly drab by comparison.

Alan chuckled. 'I'm sure Charles II would have approved! But I must admit, you don't get parties like this too often. It's probably a tax dodge.'

The room was thickly carpeted, and a bar, glittering with glasses and bottles, ran the whole length of one side. The far wall was one vast mirror right to the ceiling, reflecting the sparkle of chandeliers that hung like baubles on a giant Christmas tree. On the side opposite the bar a band played subtle and highly professional modern jazz, and already one or two people were dancing, moving their bodies with a kind of self-conscious precision that suggested they were only doing it to be noticed.

From the confusion of the crowd, suddenly Anna Loriot appeared like a small tornado. She was glorious in nothing but black, a dress that had probably been in her wardrobe since the 1930s and was embroidered all over with tiny jet beads. She waved a glass at Cassie and Alan.

'*Mes enfants!* Come, join us! We are all here to eat and drink as much of Van's money as we can, so don't be shy.' She gave Alan a huge wink, and he laughed.

'How can I refuse an offer like that? Come on, Cass, let's get started.'

Cassie raised her eyebrows. Alan had a look on his face that she knew of old—he was determined to enjoy himself tonight, and that probably meant getting happily drunk. Luckily, though, Alan took drink well; where some men got belligerent and nasty, he was more likely to laugh and dance and crack jokes—all harmless fun.

They battled through the throng and reached the bar, where Van Hamer was sitting on a high stool and watching the party with a small smile on his face. For a moment Cassie felt uneasy—there was something unhealthy about his expression, as if he were a wolf on a hill watching a flock of grazing sheep and waiting to pounce. She pushed the fancy aside with a small shiver and ordered a vodka and orange juice. As the barman scooped ice into her glass she turned to speak to Alan, but found that someone else had beaten her to it. A dark-haired girl, dressed flamboyantly in red, had glided up to him and was talking in a high-pitched voice punctuated with a lot of hand-waving. A cigarette in a holder dangled from one long-taloned hand, and the other was slowly but surely making its way along the top of the bar towards Alan's elbow. She had huge, hungry eyes, and with a secret grin Cassie summed her up—a bit-part actress with big ambitions. She's probably spent all day working out her plan: introduce herself to the director, chat him up and, later, suggest a little private tête-à-tête, then knock him flat with her irresistible charm. She would only be the first of many, and though he knew what her motive must be, Alan loved flattery. He was going to have a whale of a time this evening.

Suddenly, Cassie decided to have a little fun herself. Reaching out, she let her fingers curl round Alan's arm and said sweetly, 'Won't you introduce me, Alan?'

Alan turned to look at her, and she saw laughter in his eyes. The girl in red scowled. 'Yes,' Alan said, 'this is—I'm sorry, I've forgotten your name...'

The scowl became deeper. 'Andrea.'

'Andrea, of course. This is Cassie. My personal assistant.'

The hungry eyes raked Cassie up and down, and Andrea said coldly, 'Pleased to meet you. Alan, as I was saying about that TV play I did—'

Cassie left it at that. Poor Alan—it wasn't fair to spoil his fun just for the sake of a joke. Turning back to the bar she sipped at her drink, listening to the waves of music and chatter that swelled around her. Quite a lot more people were dancing now, and she watched them, content just to sit and observe for the time being. Despite the fact that the real work was yet to start, the last few days had been pretty hectic. There had been conferences, meetings, discussions between Alan, the scriptwriter and the principal actors about last-minute changes, last-minute location problems to overcome. Cassie felt as though she'd never worked so hard in her life. Everything was on such a big scale with this film—it was make or break now, and she knew that over the next few weeks the pressure would really be on. It might be a good idea to have one over the eight herself tonight, just to make herself relax.

She finished her drink, allowed the barman to refill her glass, then moved away across the room to watch the dancers more closely. There seemed to be a particularly large knot of people in one corner, surrounding someone she couldn't see and, curious, she headed towards them. Then, on the edge of the gaggle, she stopped and smiled. Guy Carver. She should have known. He was talking to his agent, Andrew Symes, and beside him stood a petite girl with corn-fair hair that hung nearly to her waist. At first glance she looked light-hearted and confident, but when Cassie looked closer she could see some tell-tale signs. The girl shifted uncomfortably from one foot to the other and was clearly trying to look as though she belonged. But her face gave her away. There were heavy shadows under her carefully made up eyes, and the eyes themselves—well, Cassie could only describe them as haunted. Behind the mask, she was miserable—and it was easy to see why.

This was obviously the latest in Guy Carver's long string of conquests, and Cassie guessed that her reign wasn't going to last much longer. Guy was literally besieged by women, all simpering at him, all trying to capture his attention, all eager to be the next in line. And he was holding court like a king. Even as Cassie watched, he reached out a hand to trace a playful line down the chin and neck of one of his admirers while she laughed at some remark he had made. The light in his vivid grey eyes was calculating and amused, and suddenly Cassie experienced a wave of contempt for him. He treated these women like cattle, looking them over while he decided which one he would grant a favour to next. And as for the little blonde at his side...she would be just another name in his old diaries before long.

Suddenly Guy caught sight of Cassie. Immediately he waved. 'Well, if it isn't the perfect secretary! How are you enjoying the party, Cassie?'

She would have liked to pretend she hadn't heard, but it was too late. Forcing a smile she walked towards him. 'Very much, thanks.'

The grey eyes flicked over her figure. 'You look great.' And, seeing her face, he added in an undertone that the others couldn't hear, 'No, I mean it. Very fresh and cool. It makes a pleasant change.'

The blonde girl gave her an uncomfortable, resigned look, and she stepped a pace away from Guy, trying to show that she wasn't interested in him. One of the other women grabbed Guy's arm and said, 'Darling, they're playing my favourite number. *Do* dance with me—you're such a *lovely* dancer!'

Guy smiled—a synthetic smile if ever there was one—and let her pull him away. The blonde girl stared after them sadly, and Cassie said, 'I'm Alan Blythe's assistant, by the way. I don't think we've met before, have we?'

The girl started like a nervous kitten and said, 'No...no, we haven't. My name's Sophie.' She was still gazing after Guy.

Cassie decided to jump in at the deep end. She felt

very sorry for Sophie; she was obviously having a hard time, yet was too afraid of losing Guy to protest. Sympathetically she leaned forward and said in the girl's ear, 'Trouble?'

Sophie blinked. 'You could say that. I wish I hadn't come tonight. Not that it would have made any difference.' Then she turned to face Cassie fully. 'But there's no point telling you all about it, is there? Why should it matter to you? It's my business.' And with that she walked away, leaving Cassie feeling embarrassed.

Well, she'd tried. And she couldn't blame Sophie for taking the attitude she had. Peering through the crowd she saw Guy dancing with the other girl, who was moving her body outrageously, trying to excite him, and suddenly Cassie would have loved to claw her eyes out, for Sophie's sake. Or maybe Guy himself should be the target—certainly he was leading the girl on, and it wouldn't be surprising if they 'disappeared' together before long. Disgusted, Cassie went back towards the bar to see how Alan was getting on.

Guy didn't disappear with his new partner. Instead, he discarded her after half an hour and was soon back amid a bevy of girls. For a while Sophie tagged along behind him, but as the night wore on Cassie saw her alone at the bar, drinking bacardis in quick succession and trying desperately to maintain the illusion that she was enjoying the party. She didn't attempt to speak to her again.

To her own surprise, Cassie found that she too was in demand. She had not realized how many male hangers-on, as well as female, existed in the film world, and as soon as word got around that she was the director's assistant she was approached by a succession

37

of men who wanted to dance with her and get her drinks in the hope that she would introduce them to Alan. She brushed each one off politely but coolly, privately thinking that they were in their own way every bit as bad as their female counterparts.

Shortly before midnight Alan found her. He had a giggling girl on each arm, and his face was flushed.

'Hi! Having fun?' he asked.

'Great.' She raised her glass, grinning at him. 'So are you, by the look of it.'

'I'll have a grandmother of a hangover in the morning, but right now I'm past caring. Be seeing you!' And he weaved away.

Dear old Alan, Cassie thought. He was like a schoolboy let loose in a vast toyshop—so much to choose from, he didn't know where to start. Unlike Guy, who led them on and teased them and dropped them with such careless ease.

She felt suddenly uncomfortable. Guy was the last person she wanted to think about, yet his behaviour tonight was preying on her mind for reasons she couldn't fathom. He angered her more than he should have done, and that was something she didn't like, because it hinted that she had a reason to be angry. Why should she care what he did? He was like most of the other people here—phoney. And Cassie always did her best to avoid phoneys...

Oh, to hell with it. Ordering another drink (how many was this? She was beginning to feel light-headed) she concentrated her attention on her favourite game of the night—watching other people. Nearly everyone was now dancing, while the tireless band played on. They were losing their inhibitions and the masks were starting to slip, but she felt detached from it all. She would never have the sort of money that these Beautiful People were used to, and even if she had, she wouldn't have their inbuilt instinct for how to spend it. Which was probably just as well, as she didn't want to end up like them—as an insincere shell.

Whoops, Cassie, watch it! she thought, checking herself. This wouldn't do—she was getting self-righteous, and that was a sure sign that she'd had one too many. After all, whatever she might think of them, she wasn't exactly God's gift to the world either...

'I've been watching you.'

The voice made her jump, and she turned to see Guy standing behind her. He seemed stone-cold sober. A small smile played around his mobile mouth, and for once he was alone. 'You've not been dancing. Don't you dance?'

'Yes, sometimes.'

He held out a hand, taking hers firmly. 'Then let's put that right. Come on, and I won't listen to any arguments.'

Well, she thought, there was no harm in it. She followed him across the floor. The band had started a slow tune, and she was nonplussed when Guy's arm curved round her waist, drawing her close to him. She caught a faint scent of something amberish, but it wasn't after-shave; it was more natural...pleasant.

'Relax,' he said in her ear. 'We're all here to have fun, and I'm not going to eat you.'

She laughed self-consciously, realizing that she had tensed her body as he took hold of her. He was a good dancer, his movements easy and fluid, and the hand that held hers was dry and warm with a firm, decisive grip. Glancing up at his face she saw that he was staring into the middle distance, a small frown creasing his brow under the black hair. Yes, she could see why he was so successful with women. Under the sophistication there was a kind of little-boy-lost air about him, when he let it show through. That, coupled with his arrogance, would present a challenge that most girls couldn't hope to resist. They all wanted to be the one to tame him, to get through the outer shell to the soft heart underneath. *Soft heart my foot,* she told herself.

'Are you enjoying it?' His voice broke into her reverie and she wondered whether he was referring to the party in general, or just this moment.

'Very much.' He could take that however he pleased.

'I suppose you're as used as I am to this sort of thing.'

'No, I'm not. I don't usually go to the big parties they hold back home, and when I do they're not on such a grand scale.' She shrugged. 'I suppose it isn't really in my league.'

Guy gave her an odd look but didn't comment. For a minute or two, they danced without speaking, then he said almost absently, 'You're a very good mover.'

Was he being deliberately ambiguous? Cassie decided to give him the benefit of the doubt. 'So are you,' she said.

He gave a quick, sharp laugh that startled her. 'You have to have all the social graces in my line of country. The fans don't like it if their heroes turn out to be anything less than perfect.'

She was surprised by the remark, and observed, 'That sounds very cynical.'

'Does it? Yes, I suppose it does.' And, infuriatingly, he said no more.

The dance ended, and Cassie made to move back. But Guy's arm stayed around her waist and she found

40

herself still close to him. He looked down at her and his eyes were suddenly overbright, unfathomable.

'What's the matter?' he said drily. 'Afraid I'm going to throw you over my shoulder and bear you off to my den?'

'No.' She laughed, embarrassed, and forced herself to relax in his grasp. Out of the corner of her eye she thought she glimpsed Sophie watching them. Impulsively, she added, 'But I don't think your girlfriend's too happy about you dancing with me.'

Guy's expression darkened. 'Her opinion doesn't interest me, so I don't see why it should bother you.'

That, she thought, was typical of him, and suddenly she wished she hadn't accepted the invitation to dance in the first place. Angry, she retorted, 'Well, it does. I don't believe in upsetting people unnecessarily.'

Abruptly Guy released her, and the familiar mask-like indifference returned to his face. 'I see. I didn't realize you were such a staunch champion of the underdog.' There was heavy sarcasm in his tone. 'Though if you really think that Sophie and her kind are underdogs, you've got quite a lot to learn.' And, taking her hand again in a cool grip, he made a mock bow over it. 'Thank you for the dance, Miss MacRae. I hope you enjoy the rest of the party.'

He turned and walked away, and Cassie was left staring at his departing back as he headed for the bar, with Sophie hurrying in his wake.

The party turned sour for Cassie after that. Guy had succeeded in infuriating her to the point where she couldn't enjoy herself, and within half an hour she decided to call it a night. She was feeling very tired by this time anyway, and the idea of going to her room and ordering a late cup of coffee to drink in bed appealed to her. So she left the Charles II suite and walked down the corridor to the lifts. She stabbed the 'call' button, and when the lift arrived pressed for the ninth floor—or thought she did. Her mind was racing indignantly from the sharp encounter with Guy, and she hadn't concentrated on what she was doing, so that when the lift door opened again and she stepped out, she was in fact not on the ninth floor, but the eighth.

She did not realize at first that she had made a mistake, but made her way along the passage. Only when she noticed that the room numbers were wrong did she stop, and the truth dawned on her.

'Damn!' she muttered under her breath. Well, there wasn't much point in recalling the lift; she might as well find the stairs and climb up to the next floor—it would be quicker. She walked on towards the staircase, but as she passed by a door that stood half open, a vaguely familiar voice drifted out of the room beyond, making her pause.

Where had she heard those smooth and slightly oily tones before? She searched her memory . . . Of course! It was Van Hamer's voice. He was talking low and quickly to someone, and Cassie's curiosity was aroused. She didn't make a habit of listening at keyholes, but this wasn't a keyhole—the door was open and anyone could have overheard. And just now, she was sure, she had heard Van Hamer mention Alan.

Suddenly cautious, she tiptoed to a position where she could peep into the suite without being seen from within. Yes, it was Hamer—and with him was Guy's agent, Andrew Symes.

'Of course not,' Hamer was saying. 'That's not

going to be a problem. It's just a matter of sorting out a few last details.'

Symes nodded. 'And keeping Guy Carver out of it, of course.'

Out of what? Cassie wondered. Then Hamer spoke again.

'That's your department, not mine. But be careful—we've got to make damned sure that neither Carver nor Blythe starts getting suspicious, or we'll have big problems.'

Cassie drew in her breath sharply. *Suspicious?* She didn't like the sound of that one little bit. Craning closer, she was startled when Symes said, 'Hold on a minute, Van. Shouldn't you close that door?'

Van Hamer turned to face the door, and Cassie drew back swiftly. She heard him say, 'You're being paranoid, Andrew. But if it makes you happy, all right.' He started towards her, and hastily she dodged back, looking over her shoulder for somewhere to hide. The last thing she wanted was to be seen.

To her relief there was a side corridor which led off the main passage, and she ducked into it a second before the producer put his head out of the suite door and looked right and left. She heard him call back to Symes, 'Okay, no KGB in sight!' And the door was firmly closed.

Cassie leaned back against the wall. *What was going on in there?* She would have loved to eavesdrop again, but these hotel doors were solid and the chances of overhearing anything else were very slim. She left her hiding place and headed for the stairs to return to her own room, where she ordered coffee. Then, when it arrived, she sat back on the bed and thought over what she had heard.

43

It sounded as if Van Hamer and Symes were hatching some plot together that, while having something to do with the film, had nothing to do with its cast or director. Or maybe 'hatching a plot' was the wrong way to put it—that made it sound as if something illegal or at least underhand was going on. But certainly they had seemed very anxious to keep it secret from Alan and Guy, and from the way they were talking they were clearly afraid of being found out. From the moment she first saw him Cassie had neither liked nor trusted Van Hamer, and Andrew Symes was made of the same stuff—very confident, very slick, and altogether too pleasant to be true. So what were they up to? It was a pity she'd not been able to hear the rest of their conversation, as the little she had learned wasn't enough to make it worthwhile telling anyone. They would just dismiss it as a meaningless snippet. And yet she felt she ought to alert Alan, as whatever was afoot clearly concerned him in some way.

She drank some more of the coffee, feeling the hot liquid clearing her head. There was no point sitting here brooding about it; she couldn't draw any conclusions, and if she let her imagination run away with her, goodness knows where it might lead. Best to try and forget about it for the moment. But as she undressed and went into the bathroom to have a shower, she made one resolution. She would keep a sharp eye on Van Hamer—and at the first sign of anything else suspicious, she would tell Alan exactly what she had discovered.

4

From that time on, Cassie had little chance to worry about Van Hamer and his intrigues. The next day was a Sunday, and she woke late, finding when she did finally leave her room that Alan was up and away—probably thoroughly enjoying himself looking around London. In fact the entire hotel seemed quiet: most of the film's cast and crew, aware that this was their last free day before work began, were making the most of it. And that, Cassie thought, was a cue for her to do likewise.

It was only a pity that the West End shops were all closed. Ever since the project had been first mooted, and she had known that she would be coming to England, she had planned a mammoth shopping spree in London. Today though, all she would be able to do would be to look in the windows. On the other hand, she reflected, that could be just as well—although she'd saved quite a bit of money for her spending spree, her resources were still very limited and she knew how easy it would be to give in to temptation and wave goodbye to an awful lot of cash.

However, she decided nonetheless to spend the afternoon strolling around Mayfair and window-shopping. The weather had improved and was quite bright, though still cold, and after a light lunch in the hotel she was about to set off when she met Anna Loriot in the lobby.

'Cassie!' The Frenchwoman hailed her in a voice that turned every head in earshot. '*Chérie,* I want to speak to you!'

Anna was resplendent in gold and amber today, with a necklace of gigantic topazes glittering at her neck. For one brief moment Cassie thought she looked out of place in this world of the late twentieth century—how much better she would have fitted into the high-glamour era of the 1930s!

'*Chérie!*' Anna strode towards her, reaching out a hand to take Cassie's in a possessive, motherly grip. 'Alan tells me that as well as your other work you are to be our *chaperon* when we are not on set, is that not so?'

Cassie smiled doubtfully. 'Well, I'm not sure about that exactly . . . but he has asked me to help out where I can.'

'To look after the cast and be the ministering angel outside of working hours? *Bien!* Then you can begin by being my guest tonight!'

'Your guest . . . ?' Cassie didn't quite understand.

'*Oui, ma chérie!* Tonight I dine out at the one restaurant in London where it is possible to have a tolerable cuisine. A little indulgence before we all put the noses to the grindstone! And you are my guest.'

Cassie opened her mouth, not quite sure if she could face the prospect of living it up in style the night before filming began, but before she could say a word Anna swept on relentlessly, 'Do not give me the argument, because I will not hear it! You have not yet had time to find yourself an *amour* in London, so there is no excuse for having another engagement! It is settled! At eight o'clock we meet here in the foyer, yes?'

46

Cassie could only give in gracefully. With a warm smile, she said, 'Yes—and thank you very much. It'll be lovely.'

Anna looked pleased with herself. Saying, 'At eight, then!' she turned and was about to walk away when an afterthought struck Cassie.

'Oh, Anna—how should I dress?'

The actress looked over her shoulder and beamed. 'Ah, a young woman who still knows how to observe the graces! In my day every girl asked that question, and properly so: but now—ah, they do not care! You are very refreshing, *chérie*, and I say to you—be like the peacock. Tonight we shall be in style!'

And with that she was gone.

With a smile Cassie went on her way. Now that she had been railroaded into this, she realized that it could well turn out to be a marvellous evening. Anna was highly entertaining company, and there certainly wouldn't be much time for socializing over the next few weeks. On a professional note, she reflected also that Alan would be pleased to see her getting on well with Anna Loriot—it would help to smooth his path with the temperamental actress. Yes; all in all, she felt, tonight would do her a lot of good all round.

But if she had known the full details of what Anna was planning, she might have looked forward to the evening with a few misgivings.

Cassie thoroughly enjoyed her afternoon. In one way, the fact that the shops were all closed was highly frustrating, but in another it came as a relief. She saw so many clothes, accessories and other beautiful articles in the Mayfair windows that she knew she wouldn't have been able to resist, and all at what seemed to be extortionate prices. She knew full well that her chequebook would never have stood the strain. Nevertheless, it *was* torture to be able only to look, and she promised herself a second visit to many of the shops as soon as the opportunity came her way.

After a couple of hours, deciding that she couldn't stand the frustration any longer, she left the shopping streets and went for a walk in Hyde Park. She was beginning to change her mind about England; even here in the middle of the capital city everything was so incredibly green, and the sense of bustle even in the park on a Sunday appealed to her. She walked as far as Kensington Gardens, and was fascinated by the cross-section of people she encountered. Then, as the afternoon began to chill, she made her way back to the hotel.

She had been intending to have a quiet word with Alan about the conversation she had overheard between Van Hamer and Andrew Symes, but found on her return that there was still no sign of him. She had coffee sent to her room, and after drinking it and watching (despite her determination not to) an episode of a Sunday children's serial on television, she realized that she would have to start getting ready.

She had a leisurely bath, washed her hair, and while she dried it looked through her wardrobe, which depressed her. Her one really elegant dress—the grey silk—she had worn last night at the party; she couldn't wear it again so soon, not with such an exacting hostess as Anna, whose ideas of dress sense were thoroughly uncompromising. And most of her other things were too casual...

She finally, though a little doubtfully, selected a dark red dress which wasn't in itself anything remarkable, but which could be pepped up by a few well-chosen accessories. For more than half an hour

48

Cassie stood in front of the mirror trying first one thing and then another, and finally decided to wear a silky black shawl over the dress, which made it look a bit more dramatic, a narrow black belt, and a black velvet choker at her neck. It was the best she could do, and with black tights and shoes she thought it would pass muster. And so at eight o'clock she stepped out of the lift on the hotel's ground floor.

Anna, as usual, was late, and for a few minutes Cassie wandered around the foyer trying not to feel conspicuous. At last, when she was wondering whether it would be worth her while snatching a quick drink at the bar to build up her confidence, the little French-woman appeared.

'Cassie! I keep you waiting—forgive me! An old woman's indulgence; at my age, I am allowed to be late.'

Cassie smiled. 'Don't worry, Anna. You look *lovely!*'

Anna was indeed a vision, this time swathed from head to foot in almond green and silver, and her appearance quite alarmed Cassie, making her feel drab. But Anna looked her up and down and said immediately,

'As do you, *chérie*. You have the perfect taste. Not plain; not flamboyant. You should have been born French! Now; we have only to wait for my other guest, and we shall go. I have a taxi waiting.'

Cassie was dismayed. She had had no idea that Anna had invited anyone else, and the prospect of meeting one of her friends—who would probably be as sophisticated as Anna herself—was daunting. But before she could think any more about that, Anna cried out, 'Ah! He is here!'

Cassie looked up, and felt herself freeze. Of all the

dinner companions she might have chosen for herself, Guy Carver was bottom of the list only to Van Hamer. But it was Guy Carver, devastatingly elegant in a suit that looked as though it had been moulded to his body, who was walking towards them across the foyer.

Unlike Cassie, Guy showed no surprise. He gave her a broad smile, and said, 'Hello, Perfect Secretary.'

Cassie gathered her wits together and forced herself to smile back. 'Hello. I didn't realize—'

'That I was in the party? No, I thought you might not. But nothing would induce me to miss out on one of Anna's treats.' He spoke lightly and cheerfully, and if the sharp words that had passed between them the night before still rankled with him, he showed no sign of it. That, at least, was something to be thankful for, Cassie told herself.

'Alan not here?' Guy asked her then, and she thought that this time there was a slight touch of sardony in his tone. But before she could reply, Anna said, 'Alan is busy,' in a voice that suggested that Alan was totally unimportant and should therefore be dismissed from the conversation. It would have been a lot easier, Cassie thought ruefully, if Alan *had* been invited, and she wondered whether Anna had deliberately left him out. She only hoped that the Frenchwoman wasn't trying to set something up between herself and Guy; if she was, that would be a big mistake.

Still, she'd have to make the best of it now. No doubt Anna's motives were sound enough; she missed very little that went on, and had no doubt seen that Cassie and Guy weren't exactly the best of friends. She probably wanted to put them on a better footing together to avoid any unpleasantness when filming started. And with that thought in mind Cassie relaxed a little. Certainly life would be a lot easier if she and Guy could patch up their differences and get along civilly. Though if he—or Anna for that matter—thought that she was going to be anything more than coolly friendly to him, they could forget it!

The taxi was waiting, its meter ticking over, outside the hotel, and so without any more delay they climbed in and were whisked off. Anna chattered about nothing in particular during the drive, which was as well as Cassie wouldn't have known where to start making conversation under the circumstances. Before long they arrived at their destination, which proved to be the sort of restaurant that Cassie had only seen before in her dreams. A dark red awning hooded the entrance, and as a doorman admitted them into an incredibly plush foyer, decorated in red and gold, its walls lined with mirrors, a small man in evening dress came to meet them. He greeted Anna in voluble French then, bowing so much that Cassie was sure he would fall over, ushered them all into the restaurant proper, which was softly lit, agleam with polished glass and filled with a gentle, muted murmur of conversation.

The restaurant was crowded. Anna later told Cassie that its clients usually had to book at least a fortnight in advance, but that she, being an old friend of the proprietor, could always get a table at a moment's notice when she was in London.

They sat down, and as Anna turned to wave to someone she knew, Guy said in an undertone to Cassie, 'Now you see why I wouldn't have missed this!'

She nodded, wide-eyed. 'You're right. It's an incredible place! The only trouble is, it makes me feel dowdy.'

He laughed softly. 'That's something you needn't

worry about.' And, seeing the sudden caution in her expression, he added, 'No, I mean it. You look very good tonight.'

Cassie made some inconsequential reply, feeling embarrassed, but luckily she was saved at that moment by a waiter who glided silently to their table and gave each of them a menu. He was followed by the proprietor, who hovered around them like an anxious mother hen, determined to see that they all chose the house's very best dishes. Cassie had no idea where to start, as everything available sounded equally tempting, so she finally allowed Anna to make the choice for her, under the owner's guidance. Wine was brought, and before long the meal was under way.

The food was magnificent. Cassie felt that she could have gone on eating all night just to savour the exquisite taste of everything. She was careful, though, not to drink too much—after all, they all had an early start in the morning, and she at least had to set a good example.

As the evening wore on, both she and Guy relaxed. She had been embarrassed during the early stages by the fact that people at other tables tended to stare at them—obviously Guy and Anna had been recognized, and Cassie knew that the other diners were sizing her up, and had probably presumed she was Guy's latest conquest. That irritated her—she had no wish at all to be linked with him, even if it was only in the minds of a few people, and it wasn't until they had finished their dessert and ordered coffee that she was able to put the annoyance out of her mind.

To her dismay Anna then rose. 'My dears, you will excuse me one moment?' she said with a smile. 'There is a very old friend of mine across the room, and I would like very much to speak with her. I shall be back in the trice!'

Guy watched her as she swept across the room, turning heads, then he laughed. 'Dear Anna!' he said. 'She's so transparent in some ways, isn't she?'

'Is she?' Cassie knew exactly what he meant, and she was a little annoyed with Anna for her obvious attempt at match-making, but she was determined not to let Guy know that.

'She wants us to be friends,' Guy said with amusement. 'So; what are friends supposed to talk about over the dinner table?'

'As far as I'm aware, real friends don't need to think up topics of conversation,' Cassie replied. 'It's supposed to happen naturally.'

'Like a lot of other things.'

She looked sharply at him. 'Probably.'

Already the atmosphere was beginning to turn sour, and Cassie knew that it was her own fault. The trouble was, she was so wary of this man—she couldn't deny his attraction, and yet she was as determined as ever not to like him. If only he wouldn't smile at her in that patronizing way, she thought, she would find it a lot easier to be pleasant. But always he managed to ruffle her; she could almost feel her defensive hackles rising now.

With an effort she forced herself to smile properly at him. 'It's a shame Alan wasn't around,' she said. 'He'd have loved this.'

Guy's eyes narrowed. 'Oh, so Alan's to be the topic of conversation, is he? Yes, it is a pity.' He sounded about as insincere as it was possible to be. Then, with a distinct barb in his voice, he added, 'You could have brought him to chaperon you, and I could have brought

Sophie to chaperon me. That would have been a cosy party.'

Cassie bridled and she retorted, 'I wasn't aware that anyone needed a chaperon.'

'Neither was I. It was your suggestion, if you recall. Or is it that you don't feel happy without Alan to back you up?'

That, she thought furiously, was vicious. 'I'm quite confident enough on my own, thank you,' she told him sharply. 'But I happen to enjoy Alan's company.'

Guy looked down at his empty glass, and refilled it. Witheringly, he said, 'I'm sure you do.'

Thankfully, before the siutation could get any worse, Anna returned. She saw at once that her two companions weren't exactly getting along like brother and sister, and her face clouded.

'*Mes enfants!* You are not enjoying yourselves?'

They both protested that they were, and over coffee both made an effort to keep up a façade of cheerfulness. Anna was grimly determined that nothing should spoil her treat, and as she did most of the talking the atmosphere had eased quite a lot by the time the bill was paid and the moment came to leave.

But then, in the taxi that had been called for them, Anna dropped a bombshell.

'My dears, the night is young, and I am not so old—I have a fancy to go on to a nightclub I know.' She whispered a name in Guy's ear, and he smiled.

'Yes, why not?'

Cassie started to say that she would much prefer to go back to the hotel, but Anna would hear none of it. She was in London, and it was her duty to see and do as much as she could. And so, her protests having got her nowhere, she was whisked in the direction of Piccadilly.

Anna was normally a very subtle woman, but to-night her sensitivity seemed to have completely deserted her, for when they arrived at the club, she suddenly announced that she had a headache.

'I cannot face the heat and the noise,' she said. 'A great shame, for I was much looking forward to it! But there—you two shall go, and you shall have a good time for me.'

Guy and Cassie, who were already out of the taxi, looked dismayed, but before either of them could say a word, Anna had shut the cab door firmly and waved the driver on. The car pulled away, leaving them standing together on the pavement.

Inwardly, Cassie was seething. However well intentioned Anna might be, she had put her in an impossible position. To go with Guy Carver into a night-club? At that moment, she thought she'd rather have swum home to Sydney!

Guy, however, seemed unperturbed. 'Well,' he said calmly, 'shall we go in?'

'I—think I'd rather not. Anna didn't give me a chance to say anything, but I *am* very tired.' It was a lame excuse, and he knew it. He frowned.

'Worried that Alan might be waiting up for you and worrying?' he said tartly.

That did it. Cassie snapped back, 'No. I'm worried that anyone who sees me in there with you might get the wrong impression.'

Guy looked furious, and she guessed that no woman had ever spoken to him like that before. One thing his ego couldn't take was the idea that any girl would rather be somewhere else than with him.

'Well, you needn't worry about that,' he retorted. 'There'll be enough talent in there to keep you happy, however fussy you are. And if you're afraid I'm going to hang on to your hand once we get inside, forget it!'

Cassie gave him an icy smile. 'That just about sums you up, doesn't it?' she said. 'Well, you go right ahead. Find some dumb female to fall for your line of chat and your famous name, and have lots of fun! Personally, I prefer my own company!'

It was an incredible stroke of good luck that when she turned around, intending to walk away, a taxi was cruising down the street towards her with its light on. She hailed it, and as it pulled up she scrambled in.

'The Albury Hotel, please,' she said to the driver. Damn Guy and his arrogance, and damn Anna and her matchmaking! She'd have to apologize to the Frenchwoman, of course, but she knew that Anna would understand. She had done her best, but her efforts had been misguided. And as for Guy . . .

She knew she was more angry than she should have been, but told herself that it was justified. Maybe she had been rude to Guy, but he'd asked for it, and had been asking for it since the day they met. Now she had made her point, made her position quite clear, and if they were enemies from tonight on, well, at least the relationship would be honest.

And that funny feeling at the back of her mind, that nagging, disturbing little upset, was just her imagination she decided. She *wasn't* unhappy, and she *didn't* regret losing her temper, because she *did not* like Guy Carver. And that, she thought fiercely, was an end to it.

5

There was no trace of Alan in the hotel when she returned, and Cassie guessed that he must either still be out or have returned early and gone to bed. Anna, too, had retired, which was just as well, as Cassie was still boiling from her fracas with Guy, and didn't want to have to explain it all. She crawled gratefully into her bed, and was asleep within minutes.

And when her alarm shrilled at five a.m., the brief holiday was over.

A car arrived for herself and Alan at 6:30, before which she spent a hectic hour checking that nothing had been forgotten and that everyone knew where they had to be and when. The first day's footage was to be shot in a quiet area of the Thames's south bank, and on the journey there Cassie was intrigued by the London sights they passed, even having a distant glimpse of the Tower.

She was feeling a little under the weather this morning—a heavy meal and a few glasses of wine, coupled with less sleep than she would have liked, had taken their toll. And she was not looking forward to encountering Guy again. Not only that, but she would have to face Anna with the story of what had happened after her departure, and Anna, she knew, would be none too pleased.

But when the car drew up on the site, she smiled and relaxed. It was all so familiar—no matter whereabouts in the world she might travel, a film set was always a film set—the same confusion and chaos of caravans, caterers, huge batteries of lights and, everywhere, mile upon mile of snaking cables to trip over. At last Cassie felt at home.

A small section of the riverbank had been sealed off from the public to avoid the problem of gawpers, and technicians and administrative staff scurried about like ants. It always astonished Cassie to think that a complete film could ever come out of such total mayhem.

Alan was also a little the worse for wear this morning—he had confided to Cassie in the car that he had visited several pubs the previous night, with the assistant director and the scriptwriter, and his eyes were heavy and somewhat bloodshot. He had questioned Cassie about her own evening, but she had been evasive, only saying that she had eaten out with Anna and Guy, at Anna's invitation. Alan suspected there was more to it than met the eye, but was in no condition to probe too far—and besides, he had more immediate things on his mind.

It was Cassie's first job to ensure that everyone was where they should be, and for half an hour after arriving she checked the wardrobe and makeup departments, spoke to the continuity girl, moved a couple of cars which were parked in the wrong place and kept Alan supplied with strong black coffee. All the cast—with the exception of Anna Loriot—had arrived, and when she stepped into the makeup caravan she came face to face with Guy Carver, who was being attended to by the tall, strong-faced woman in charge.

Guy looked coldly at her and nodded. 'Good morning.'

She had no answer. 'Morning,' she said distantly; then, 'Is everything all right?'

His eyes seemed to search her face, but gave away nothing of what he was thinking. 'Yes, thanks,' he said at length; then; 'You look very professional this morning.'

Damn you, she thought, and replied frostily, 'That's the general idea.'

'None the worse for wear?' His smile was not particularly humorous.

'Unlike you, I had a relatively early night.'

'Yes, so you did. You really put me to shame.'

The makeup woman smiled behind her hand, and Cassie turned on her heel and left the caravan. She would go back later, when Guy had gone—right now, she was in no mood for another needle-match with him.

Crossing towards the mobile wardrobe, she saw a large Daimler limousine with darkened windows drawing up beside Alan's car, and moments later Anna Loriot climbed out with slow, easy grace. She was half an hour late, but behaved as if she had all the time in the world. And when she saw Cassie she waved and beckoned.

Oh-oh, Cassie thought. She forced a smile as she hurried towards the Frenchwoman.

'Anna!' she said, 'I'm afraid I owe you an apology.'

But to her surprise Anna dismissed this, saying, 'No, no, *chérie*, it is I who must apologize! Last night I made the *faux pas*—it was very embarrassing for you, and I am sorry.'

Glancing round to make sure they were not overheard, she added, 'I saw Guy this morning, and demanded that he tell me what happened. You had an argument?'

'You could put it like that, I suppose,' said Cassie.

'*Tiens!* Well, it is the fault of a silly old woman! I wanted merely for you to get along nicely together, as I had seen how you went like the cat and dog at the party. But I should not have tried to throw you together. It was a mistake.' She smiled impishly. 'Am I forgiven, *chérie?*'

Cassie laughed. 'Anna, there's nothing to forgive! We just—don't get on, that's all.'

The Frenchwoman shrugged resignedly. 'Ah, so it would seem. Well, we shall have to see. But in the meantime, Cassie, as a big favour to me, please try to smile at him once in a while, *hein?* He is so impossible to work with if he is in the bad temper!'

'I'll try,' Cassie promised, thinking privately that Alan would soon be making the same plea if there were any more rows.

'Good! And now I must go to work or Alan shall fire me!'

An hour later, the filming began. As the cameras started to roll Cassie allowed herself to relax for the first time since waking. At last she had a few minutes with nothing to do, and she found herself a chair well out of the way of Alan and the crew, and sat down to watch for a while.

Guy Carver and Anna Loriot were playing a brief scene together—a heartrending moment when the ageing singer and the penniless young musician confronted each other with their emotions and fears—and as she watched, Cassie had to admit to herself that

Guy was good—more than good; he was superb. He gave his role just the right touch of pathos without overdoing it, and acting opposite the incomparable Anna seemed to bring out the best in him. For a few minutes he *was* the character he played. All traces of the cynical womaniser were gone, and Cassie had to remind herself forcibly that this new and much softer personality was only a pretence. But if he could convince *her* with his performance, little wonder that he was so irresistible to other women...

She shook her head almost dazedly as an aircraft roared overhead, the sound-man swore under his breath and Alan called to everyone to cut and start again. Guy strolled over to him and said something, then, seeing Cassie, winked. She turned away, annoyed that he had caught her looking at him.

They shot the scene again, and this time Anna was not concentrating and forgot one of her lines. The third time was passable, Alan decided, but they would film it once more, 'just for luck.'

And so it continued until one o'clock, when with a thankful sigh everyone stopped for lunch. A queue began to form at the large catering caravan, and Cassie, enticed by the smell of fried chicken, joined it. Alan was deep in conversation with the chief lighting technician, so to avoid getting in his way she went to sit near the river, where she could watch the dark glide of the water.

Five minutes later, Guy Carver came to join her.

She had heard someone approaching, and when she turned round and saw who it was, she froze.

He nodded in his characteristic way, then said, 'Are we on speaking terms at the moment? I'm not quite sure of the rules of etiquette here.'

Cassie shrugged. 'I'm on speaking terms if you are. We can't very well refuse to talk to each other professionally.'

'No, of course we can't. All right, a cease-fire exists! Do you mind if I sit down?'

'Help yourself.'

He did, then said, 'Taking a breather?'

She looked at him under lowered lashes. 'I can't call it that—I've hardly done anything all morning.'

He grimaced. 'I wish I could say the same! I feel like some kind of a gargoyle with this makeup—I think the woman overdid it.'

Cassie shook her head. 'Wait till you see the rushes,' she told him. 'You'll have just the right look of haggard poverty.'

The brilliant grey eyes flickered across her face, as if he was trying to decide whether she had been joking, or subtly insulting. 'Thanks a lot! I'm glad you're not my publicity agent.'

'I'd never stand the pace.' She ate another forkful of chicken and speared a couple of chips to go with it.

There was a pause, and then Guy said, 'Look, if this *is* a cease-fire, I'd just like to say I'm sorry about last night.'

Cassie stopped eating and looked warily at him. 'There's no need to say anything.'

'Maybe not, but I want to.'

Slowly then she nodded. 'In that case . . . I'm sorry too.' She hesitated, then decided there was no harm in being honest. 'Frankly, I was a bit annoyed with Anna. She seemed to be trying to push us together.'

'Oh, you shouldn't take any notice of that! She's just one of these people who wants everyone to adore everyone else.' He grinned, and she was taken aback by the total change in his look. 'That just isn't very realistic.'

'Well, we can agree on that, anyway!'

'I'm relieved to hear it. Can I get you a drink of some sort?'

'No, thanks.' She finished her meal and put down the plate. 'You'd be better off putting your feet up while you can. Alan's going to work everyone like slaves this afternoon.'

Guy laughed. 'And we all have to jump to attention when Alan shouts! No, don't look at me like that— I was only joking. But you really admire Alan, don't you?'

He was getting on dangerous ground, and she wasn't sure if he was unaware of it, or if he was baiting her. 'Of course I do,' she said a little stiffly. 'I wouldn't work for him otherwise.'

'*Touché*. But don't get me wrong; I admire him too. He's a good director to work with, from what I can tell. One of the best.' He smiled, and suddenly she couldn't help thinking that when he was at ease and not being aggressive or putting on a show, he had one of the most endearing smiles she had ever seen. 'And what about you? Are you starting to re-think your ideas about England?'

'Ohh . . . it could be worse. But I still keep remembering the hot sun.'

Guy laughed. 'Don't we all! Still, you'll be back home in a few months, won't you? Then you'll have the last laugh on us poor Poms.'

'I suppose so.'

He rose. 'And that will be England's loss.' He smiled again. 'I'll see you later.'

He strolled away towards the wardrobe caravan, and Cassie watched him go. She was puzzled—why

63

on earth had he sought her out today, after the ruckus between them last night? He had obviously been sounding her out, to see if she was still angry, and he had been anxious to patch up the quarrel. Good grief, he had even apologized first! She supposed that, like Anna, he wanted to avoid any unpleasantness on set, but from what she had surmised so far about him, that seemed out of character. Not only that, but she would have expected him to be smarting over the blow to his self-esteem that she had given him, and to be annoyed with her for not falling at his feet when she had the chance. On the other hand, she reminded herself that he had had very little to say once he had satisfied himself that she was prepared to forgive and forget. And he hadn't missed the chance to needle her about Alan, which was something that irritated her beyond endurance.

To hell with it, she thought. If he wanted to keep her sweet for the sake of peace and quiet, that was okay with her. Over the next few weeks she would have enough to concentrate on without worrying about Guy Carver and his motives. But although she tried to tell herself that it wasn't so, she was a little troubled—and a little intrigued.

Everyone was surprisingly satisfied with the first day's work.

Alan said to Cassie privately that evening that he could not remember ever having got off to such a smooth start on a new film, and he praised the professionalism of the actors and crew—and especially Guy Carver. Grudgingly, Cassie had to agree with him. There had been none of the expected tantrums on set, and when the day's rushes were shown at the hotel in the evening, they were excellent. Alan was certain

that this boded well for the rest of the week at least—
and events proved him right.

By Thursday, everyone was well into their stride,
and for Cassie too her daily routine had started to liven
up. She found herself doing everything from booking
restaurants for Anna, who was a noted gourmet, to
rounding up extras for a crowd scene and making a
last-minute dash to a department store to buy a re-
placement for a vital prop that one of the technicians
had broken. Everyone seemed to demand her ser-
vices—everyone, that is, except Guy.

During the days, Guy was almost conspicuous by
his absence. He worked hard, but never once asked
anyone to do anything for him—if there was anything
he wanted, he arranged it for himself. But the evenings
were different. Every night, when the day's footage
had been shown and discussed, he would seek Cassie
out, spend a few minutes chatting about nothing in
particular, and then disappear once more. She was
finding it easier to be civil to him—he no longer tried
to bait her as he had done at first—but she could not
understand why he should take the trouble to single
her out for just a few unremarkable minutes. She wondered if perhaps he was trying to break down her
barriers, teasing and tantalizing her so that she would
fall for him the way so many other women did. He
was used to being pursued, and it was quite possible,
she thought, that her studied indifference was a challenge to his conceit; a battle of wills which he couldn't
allow himself to lose. If that was the case, she decided,
he would have a long wait.

She talked about this to Alan on the Thursday evening, as they sat in the Terrace Bar sharing a bottle
of wine. But Alan, as she might have expected, only
laughed.

'You're probably right—I've seen him trying to chat you up. I'm surprised you haven't thrown your cap over the windmill for him yet.'

She scowled. 'Oh, *Alan!* He wasn't trying to chat me up! Just—talking, about nothing in particular.'

'That's how all the best relationships start,' Alan teased. 'If I were you, I'd make the most of it—most of the women in this country would scratch your eyes out for the same chance.' And, seeing her furious face, he added hastily, 'No, I'm joking, honestly—but he certainly does seem to have taken a liking to you.'

'I think it's more likely that he wants to make a conquest, on principle,' Cassie said darkly.

'Oh come on, Cass, he's not that bad! Give him the benefit of the doubt—he may actually like you.'

'Pigs might fly. I only wish he'd stop hanging around the hotel in the evenings. Why doesn't he go off to all these fantastic parties he gets invited to?'

'Ah,' Alan said, 'he wouldn't be very popular with me if he did. He's here to work as well, remember; and to give him his credit, he's a true professional. Early nights are the order now, not late rave-ups.' He leaned forward to refill her glass. 'Come on, take that scowl off your face and stop brooding about it. Anyone would think you *cared* about what Guy Carver thinks of you.'

Alan hadn't meant that last remark to be barbed, but it struck Cassie like a dart and made her feel uncomfortable. Defensively, she said, 'Well, I just don't want him to think I'm like all the others.'

Alan smiled, and let it go at that.

During most of that week, Cassie had no time to think about Van Hamer and the conversation she had overheard on the night of the party. Now that filming had started, the producer was keeping well out of the way, only turning up once or twice to see the rushes and give his approval. But on the Friday morning, something happened to remind Cassie of her resolution.

She met Alan for an early breakfast in the hotel, and when they had finished eating, he said, 'Cass, I want you to do something for me this morning. There are some papers down at Van Hamer's office that apparently came in last night—all to do with the credit and publicity clauses in our contracts—and I'd like to look them over on the set during today's lunch break. Could you be an angel and pick them up for me when the office opens?'

'Of course,' Cassie said, drinking the last of her coffee. And then she thought—*Hamer's office, I wonder . . . ?*

'It'll mean you can get an hour or two extra shut-eye—the office doesn't open till nine-thirty, and I'll let you off till then. Take a taxi both ways, on expenses.'

'My pleasure! All right, I'll see you probably at about half past ten.'

And so, at nine forty-five, a taxi drew up in the Soho sidestreet where Van Hamer's company had its offices. Walking up to reception Cassie explained her mission, and the girl at the desk looked her up and down vaguely. 'Mr. Hamer's secretary isn't in yet,' she said, studying her nails when she had finished staring at Cassie. 'But I suppose the papers are in his office somewhere. Do you want to go in and wait?'

'Yes, please. If it isn't too much trouble,' Cassie said tartly.

The receptionist shrugged. 'No trouble. Up the stairs and it's on the left. Mr. Hamer's name's on the door.'

Following directions, Cassie found the office. It was little short of opulent, dominated by a huge leather-topped desk, behind which was a vast leather swivel armchair. Various certificates hung on the walls, amid framed film posters and photographs of top stars. Cassie glanced idly around. Sheets of company notepaper lay on the desk. Looking more closely, she saw that Van Hamer wasn't, as she had thought, the absolute boss of the company. Various other names appeared on the headed paper, and it seemed that Hamer was only one director among several. Interesting... And then she saw the scribbled memo.

It said, quite simply, 'Call Symes re negotiation.' Nothing untoward there, but it reminded Cassie of her suspicions, and she turned from the desk, looking more carefully around the office.

Van Hamer's secretary had a cubby-hole that led off from the main office, and, peering through the open door, Cassie saw a line of grey filing cabinets. Could there, she wondered, be anything in them that might help her to solve the mystery of the overheard conversation?

No, she could hardly go rummaging through other people's files just on the offchance that she might find something incriminating. After all, she had nothing to go on other than a few brief sentences, and they could have meant anything. But some instinct, some feminine intuition, was nagging at her. And this was a golden opportunity; perhaps the only one she would ever have...

Quickly she crossed the room and peered out of the door, checking that no one was approaching along the corridor. Then, satisfied, she ran into the secretary's office.

She felt horribly guilty as she opened the first

drawer of the first cabinet—if anyone should catch her, she would be in real trouble, and despite the fact that she felt it was a worthy cause, she didn't like sneaking. But then she thought of Alan, and her loyalty to him won over all objections. If Hamer was out to cheat him or deceive him in any way, she was not about to stand by and let it happen.

The first drawer contained nothing of any interest, and quickly she searched through the rest of the cabinet, but again, there was nothing. The trouble was, she thought, she didn't even know what she was looking for—just a clue, a lead, something that would tell her a little more than she already knew.

And in the third cabinet, she found it.

It was a single file that had been put at the back of the bottom drawer and was marked simply, 'VH—personal'. Hastily Cassie pulled it out and opened it. And there, on the top of the file, lay a letter from Van Hamer to Andrew Symes.

The first thing Cassie noticed about the letter was that it was not written on the film company's notepaper, but instead was under Hamer's personal heading. It was typed, but to her disappointment it contained nothing that could be called incriminating. However, it was interesting enough:

Dear Andrew,
Regarding the little matter we discussed last week, I'd be grateful if you would call me at home on receipt of this letter, so that we can take things a little further. There are one or two points to be discussed which would be better handled personally rather than over the phone. I can see no reason why the transaction shouldn't go ahead as planned, and judging by the negotiations which have gone

through so far, we might be talking big money. Keep Carver on ice for the time being—if he's as anxious as you say he is to get this role, he won't see anything wrong in waiting a week or two, and the finalising of the contract is in my sole hands, so I foresee no problems there.

Yours, Van

PS Alan Blythe has been signed up as director, but we'll sort out the details of that when we come to it.

All very cryptic, Cassie thought. Though there was nothing in the letter that could really be called suspicious, she had the feeling that it had been very carefully worded. And what should the two men want to discuss that had to be tackled out of hours, on a 'personal' basis? Big money . . . and that sentence about Guy Carver on ice. What did Hamer mean, she wondered, when he said that the negotiations were in his sole hands? It was almost as though he was reassuring Symes that his fellow directors would have nothing to do with any of the contracts. And that suggested a secret which they did not want disclosed.

Frowning, Cassie started to leaf through the other papers in the file. Almost at once she came across a page of handjotted notes, mostly figures with a great number of percentage signs beside them, but there was nothing to give any clue as to what they might refer to. Then more letters, all from Hamer to Symes or vice versa. In the first, she saw a reference to Guy, but once again the letter was cryptic and cautious. But this one had a PS which she noted. It said:

'A 70/30 split between us is agreeable. Let's meet for lunch next week to discuss the next stage.'

A 70/30 split of *what?* Was it possible, she wondered with a sudden cold feeling inside her stomach, that somehow Hamer and Symes were planning to defraud the people who were working with them? Guy's name had cropped up several times already, and Alan's too. Was there some plot afoot that might cheat them of their money on this film?

No—surely that was too far-fetched. Van Hamer would never consider the idea of skipping the country with the company's funds—he had too much going for him here to make it worth his while. But something was definitely going on...

She started to look further, but suddenly from the outer office she heard the sound of a door opening and closing.

Someone was coming in! With feverish haste Cassie thrust all the letters back into the file and replaced it in its drawer.

She had just closed the drawer as quietly as possible and was straightening up when the office door opened and Van Hamer walked in.

He stopped when he saw her, and a look of surprise crossed his face. 'Miss MacRae. This is an unexpected pleasure.' His voice was smooth, cold, and his eyes seemed to bore into her as though he was only waiting for her to blush or stammer to know that he had almost caught her doing something wrong.

Cassie took a deep breath, and gave him her most pleasant smile. 'Good morning, Mr. Hamer. I'm sorry about the intrusion—I came to collect some documents that Alan wants to see today, and the receptionist said that I should wait in here. Your secretary hadn't arrived, so—'

'My secretary is at the dentist's,' he told her. 'And what exactly are the documents Alan wants?'

He was suspicious, she knew; and she prayed silently that she had not left any tell-tale signs of what she had been up to.

'Some papers that came in yesterday concerning credits and publicity,' she said. 'I don't know any more details, and as I haven't any idea what to look for, I'm afraid I've just been sitting here twiddling my thumbs.'

She must have succeeded in sounding guileless, for Hamer's narrow features relaxed a little and he almost smiled at her.

'Well,' he replied, 'I'm sorry you've been kept waiting. The papers should be in my secretary's desk—the top drawer, if you'd care to look.'

Cassie looked, and brought out a green folder. 'These?'

'That's right. I've had photocopies made, so tell Alan that he can keep them as long as he wishes. Now, is there anything else I can do for you?'

She shook her head. 'No, thank you very much. I'll be getting back to the set with these.'

He stood back to usher her into the outer office. 'If there is ever anything more you need, you only have to call me.'

Yes, Cassie thought, *rather than snoop around on your own*... The pointed hint was obvious, and she guessed that the receptionist would be in Hamer's bad books for leaving her unattended. Which suggested that he did indeed have something to hide. 'Thank you,' she said again. 'Though I don't think I'll need to trouble you.'

72

'No trouble, I assure you. Oh, and tell Alan that I'll see him at the press conference this evening, and if he wants to discuss these papers we can do it then.'

'I will.' She went out into the corridor, aware that he was watching her with his cold, small eyes, and as soon as she turned the corner she started to hurry, anxious to get out of the building as quickly as possible.

Standing on the pavement and looking for a taxi, she thought, *That was a near miss!* She had been foolish, trying to dig out Van Hamer's secrets, and she had almost been caught. And although she had succeeded in convincing him that her mission was innocent, she knew that she would not get a second chance to investigate his office while he was around. But in one sense, Van Hamer had given himself away by his reaction. Before she had only had an inkling that something was wrong. Now, though, she knew it for certain.

But that was a small consolation, for she was still faced with the problem of finding out exactly what was afoot. That would be doubly difficult now. But of one thing Cassie was certain: whatever happened, she was not going to rest until the mystery was solved.

6

The press conference that evening took place in the hotel, and by eight o'clock Cassie was rushed off her feet. She made sure that everyone who should be there knew where to go and when, showed reporters up to the suite, and rounded up one or two of the more intrepid journalists who were trying to have a look around on their own in the hope of snatching a quick exclusive interview. As well as representatives of the film trade magazines, there were also a number of writers from the national papers, and she could not help but admire Van Hamer's shrewdness in arousing so much interest in the film at this early stage. When the producer arrived with Alan, everyone quietened down and listened, taking notes as Hamer gave them a brief, smooth outline of the work that had so far been done, of their schedules, and of their expectations for the finished product. He then formally introduced Alan and the three major stars, Guy, Anna and Janey Moore, and then, with one of his insincere smiles, asked the reporters to put their questions.

As Cassie had expected, Guy and Anna were the centre of attention from then on. Anna's comeback had caused quite a stir, and for some time she was surrounded by admiring reporters who wanted to know her opinion on everything from the film to life in Paris. Anna was in her element, and played up to them with all the enthusiasm of an excited schoolgirl; although, watching her, Cassie knew that this was no more than she was used to—it was her due.

Guy, on the other hand, seemed bored by the whole thing. He was civil enough, but answered the questions put to him in as few words as possible. And when one lady journalist—who Cassie suspected was from a gossip column—started to quiz him about the more personal side of his life, he told her shortly that they were here to discuss the film, and he couldn't see that what he did in his off-duty hours had anything to do with that.

And so it went on. It was all light-hearted enough, and Alan in particular seemed to be enjoying himself immensely. But then the topic got round to money.

One of the reporters asked Guy a question. 'Mr Carver, there have been a lot of rumours flying around about the sums involved in this film—according to the grapevine, the major actors are receiving a very large fee indeed.'

'Really?' Guy replied with a slight smile.

'"Record figures" was the phrase, I think.'

'Was it?' The smile faded, and Cassie thought that Guy looked a little surprised. 'I think someone must have got their facts wrong.'

The reporter, however, was not to be put off. 'Well, can you confirm or deny the story that you, Mr. Blythe and Miss Loriot are contracted to receive a share in the profits?'

Guy's face froze momentarily, and Cassie saw Alan frown. Then Guy said, 'A percentage, you mean?'

'Yes. The rumour is—'

He was interrupted. 'Rumours have a habit of getting out of hand—as I think we all know.' A ripple of laughter, good-natured, before Guy continued, 'No, this time the rumours are wrong. Unless Anna and Alan have been hiding something from me, I can tell you now that no such deal has been negotiated.' As he spoke he looked at the other two, who shook their heads.

At that point Van Hamer rose. 'Ladies and gentlemen,' he said pleasantly—too pleasantly, Cassie thought—'I'm afraid that we shall have to call a halt to the official proceedings at this point. We all have to be up early in the morning!' He gave Alan a smile, and Alan laughed. 'Thank you all very much for your interest. If any of you would like to make your way down to the Lounge Bar on the ground floor, the company will be glad to entertain you in a less formal way.'

That, Cassie decided, was a clever trick, if English reporters were anything like their Australian counterparts. Immediately, the reporters gathered up their books and recorders, and all headed towards the door. Van Hamer and Alan went with them, and as they went Cassie saw the lady gossip-columnist moving towards Alan with a determined look. Well, he would be an easy target—if she wanted an exclusive interview, she would no doubt find it simple to charm him into giving one.

She herself hung back until the others had gone. She would have liked the chance of a private word with Alan, but there was no hope of that until the journalists had finally left the hotel. But when they had gone, she would have to see him.

Even after her furtive search of Van Hamer's office she had had doubts about whether or not her suspicions had any foundation, but now she was certain that they had. Guy had been genuinely astonished at the reporter's suggestion that he and Alan and Anna were to receive a share of the box-office takings for the film. But Cassie was experienced enough to know that even in this business there was no smoke without fire; rumours didn't start up on their own without some truth to back them up. And the way in which Van Hamer had wound up the conference so quickly and easily was telling, too. He had obviously been anxious to avoid any further questions of that sort which might have proved awkward.

So now she had her first clue. And it seemed that not only Guy and Alan but also Anna were involved in this. She could no longer give Hamer the benefit of the doubt, she decided. She had to tell someone what she knew, and what she suspected. So as soon as Alan had finished with the reporters and left the bar, she would tackle him on the subject—providing he was sober enough to listen.

She moved towards the door, lost in troubled thought, and as she stepped out of the suite a hand touched her arm, making her jump like a startled cat.

'Cassie.'

It was Guy Carver. He had been waiting outside the door, and when he saw her face, he added, 'I'm sorry, I didn't mean to scare you.'

She bridled. 'Do you make a habit of jumping out at people?'

'Sorry.' He smiled. 'But I wanted a private word.'

'Oh?' She wondered for a moment if he too suspected something odd in the way the press conference had ended so abruptly, but dismissed the idea. He had no reason to distrust Van Hamer, and unless he was telepathic, he could have no idea of what she had found out.

Guy jerked his head towards the lifts at the end of

the passage. 'The reporters have all gone off to the bar, and to be honest I've been trying to avoid them.'

'You shouldn't,' she told him. 'After all, there's nothing like a bit of publicity to help your career along.'

He grimaced. 'Maybe, but they don't want to talk about the film, and I'm not in the mood to fend off personal questions. But I would like a drink. Look— will you join me?'

His guard was down; there was none of the slightly amused bantering about him this evening. Cassie nodded. 'All right, I will, thank you. But if we go down to the ground floor, you'll be besieged. What about the Terrace Bar?'

'I'd rather not risk it. There are sure to be one or two bright lads who'll think of looking there when I don't show up in the lounge. I've got a sort of mini-suite on the tenth floor; I thought perhaps we could order a bottle of wine. It's the only place where I can really relax, unless we go out somewhere.'

She had to admit that he had a point, although she thought that by going to his rooms she would be walking right into the lion's den, which wasn't such a good idea. But if they went out to a bar somewhere, the chances were that Guy would be recognized. And even he deserved peace and quiet sometimes, she told herself with amusement.

Guy saw her hesitate, and a slightly sheepish look crossed his face. 'Believe me, you'll be quite safe,' he said, and she had the feeling that he was laughing inwardly not at her, but at himself. 'You can bring a chaperon if you want to.'

Cassie chuckled. By being straightforward with her he had got through her defences, and she could only give him best. 'All right, I trust you,' she said. 'Providing it's understood that you throw me out by eleven at the latest. I've got to be up at five-thirty.'

'Agreed.' He held out his hand, and she took it briefly, then tugged her fingers away with a smile. 'Better not. If any of the newshounds see that, the gossip pages will have a field day tomorrow.'

Guy shook his head in mock exasperation. 'Always the perfect secretary! Don't you ever go off duty?'

She looked for the sarcasm, but it wasn't there; his eyes were twinkling. 'No, I don't,' she said. 'Particularly not when I'm keeping poor overworked actors out of the clutches of the press.'

'Out of the goodness of your heart and your sense of duty.'

'Of course.'

They climbed the stairs to Guy's floor, and he ushered her into his suite. It was less sumptuous than Van Hamer's (which told her something about the film producer's priorities) but very comfortable, and Cassie sat down in a chair that stood on its own at one side of the small sitting room. Guy relaxed on the sofa opposite and lifted the telephone. Asking for room service, he ordered a bottle of white wine and two glasses, then turned to Cassie with a smile.

'Comfortable? You look uneasy.'

'No, I'm fine.' Inwardly Cassie cursed herself, but the truth was, she *was* uneasy, and beginning to doubt the wisdom of coming up here at all. Despite Alan's cheerful teasing, the fact that Guy had sought out her company so often this week bothered her; and if she was strictly honest with herself she had to admit that he was probably interested only in one thing—to get her into bed. He had reacted to the challenge her disinterest presented, and now that his first approach had failed he was having another try, but this time more subtly.

Well, let him try. It wouldn't get him anywhere— but in the meantime she might as well enjoy a glass or two of wine and a cosy chat. It was as good a way as any other of passing the time.

The wine arrived, and Guy poured. Handing her a glass he said, 'Now, what shall we drink to? And please don't say the success of the film. I've toasted that so many times in the last few days that it's starting to get very boring.'

'All right,' Cassie said. 'Here's to you then, Mr. Carver.'

'And to you, Miss MacRae! Long life, good health, and peace and quiet!' They drank, then Guy stretched his long legs out with a sigh. 'I'm going to need a holiday when all this is over. Somewhere remote, where summer's just beginning to come into full flower.'

'The Bahamas?' she suggested.

He shook his head, smiling, and one hand lightly fingered the rim of his glass, as though he were stroking a beloved pet. 'More like Wales. You've never been to Wales, have you?'

'No. This is my first time in England, remember.'

Their eyes met, and she was startled by the intensity of his expression. 'Oh, of course,' he said, and looked away. 'Soft air, mountains, rough seas, incredible scenery. I don't know whether you'd like it.'

He sounded slightly wistful, but there was a faint edge of cynicism in his voice too. Cassie shrugged, a little put out. 'I'd probably love it. You shouldn't judge everyone on first impression, you know.'

Guy looked at her again, and this time the grey eyes were hard. 'Oh, I don't know,' he replied. 'I've found it's usually a pretty safe guideline.' He drank some more wine, emptying the glass. 'Take Sophie for example. She looks empty-headed and she is empty-headed. Decorative as a Dresden shepherdess and about as useful. All glitter and glamour, with nothing underneath.'

A harsh judgement, Cassie thought. He'd probably never even taken the trouble to find out for himself if what he said was true or not, if his public treatment of Sophie was anything to go by. A little tartly, she said, 'In that case, why do you go around with her?'

The response was instant and sharp. 'I don't. Not any more. I've had more than enough of that particular lady.'

'So she's out of favour?' The words were out before Cassie could stop herself, and Guy looked angry.

'God almighty, you never give up, do you? Yes, she's out of favour, if it's anything to you. But if I wanted to talk about my personal behaviour, I'd be downstairs in the bar with all the reporters.' Now he was twisting his glass irritably between both hands. 'You don't know Sophie, so I don't think you're in a position to pass comment. Finish your wine, and let's have some more.'

Cassie reddened, aware that she had made a mistake. She had tried to be clever and Guy had put her firmly in her place. She let him pour her more wine and took refuge behind the glass, sipping from it and concentrating all her attention on it until she could calm down and stop blushing.

Suddenly she became aware that he was watching her intently. She met the gaze of his grey eyes, and he relaxed abruptly, letting his mouth curve into a wry smile.

'Sorry. I shouldn't have been so sharp with you.'

She shrugged. 'That's okay. I'm sorry, too—it was none of my business.'

'Oh, I can't blame you for being curious. Everyone else is, and I suppose on the surface it must look to you . . .' His voice tailed off, and he made a dismissive gesture with one hand. 'Never mind. Friends again?'

She nodded. 'Friends. After all, we're supposed to be having a quiet, relaxing drink.'

He looked at her again, then quickly masked the glance under his dark lashes. 'Yes, so tell me all about Australia.'

The tone of his voice was one she had heard before; he felt they should make small talk, and had said the first thing that came into his head. 'I will, if you really want to know,' she replied with a grin. 'But if you're just being polite, don't bother. Because if you do, I'll ask you to tell me all about what it's like being an actor.'

Guy laughed then; a natural laugh. 'All right, I take the point! So what shall we talk about?'

'The weather?' Cassie suggested mischievously.

'No thanks!' He paused, then, 'How about some background music? Then we don't have to talk at all if we don't want to.'

Something rang a warning bell in the back of Cassie's brain. Maybe it was a perfectly innocent suggestion, but it was also one of the oldest tricks in the book. And Guy, having played in so many romantic films, would know all about that. Still, she thought, providing he didn't play anything too obviously seductive . . .

'Fine,' she said, although there was an edge of caution in her voice.

Guy smiled, and stood up. It seemed that his suite had just about everything he could want, for there was an expensive stereo set beside the television. He switched it on and selected a cassette tape. The first strains of a Bach concerto drifted across the room, and Cassie breathed a silent sigh of relief. The music was cool, restrained and elegant—not the setting at all for a big seduction scene.

Guy didn't sit down again, but instead picked up his glass and paced across the room to the window. The curtains had been closed, but he drew them apart and stood for a few moments staring out. Then he said, half-turning, 'Have you seen the view of night-time London from up here?'

'Not really,' she admitted. 'Every time I go into my room, I'm either in a terrible hurry or desperate for some sleep.'

'You should. Come here—come and look.'

She rose and joined him at the window, and together they stood silently for a little while. The view certainly was superb. Lights twinkled almost as far as the eye could see, a glittering pattern like some vast spider's web, dominated by the futuristic and shimmering cylinder shape of the Post Office tower. Far below them in the street, cars moved like glow-worms through the light pattern. It all seemed very distant, very unreal, as though they were watching the whole spectacle on a cinema screen.

Cassie looked back towards the Post Office tower. 'That thing reminds me of a spaceship,' she said. 'I can just imagine it suddenly bursting into life and lifting off for the stars.'

Guy laughed softly. 'Funny girl,' he said; but he wasn't mocking her. And suddenly Cassie felt uncomfortable. There was an odd sensation in her spine, a tingling, as though a faint charge of static electricity had built up in the room. Her pulse was racing, and she was acutely conscious of herself.

Guy's hand touched her arm lightly, making her start. 'What's wrong, Cassie?'

She looked at him, her eyes wide and nervous. 'Nothing.'

'You shivered.'

'Did I?' She looked away. 'I'm not cold.'

'I didn't think you were.'

The words were so quiet, so gentle, that for a moment Cassie didn't catch their underlying meaning. When she did, she turned sharply to meet Guy's eyes. He didn't move, he only stood and watched her. Then he said, even more quietly, 'I was just wondering . . . what you'd do if I kissed you.'

Cassie froze. In an instant, a confusion of feelings tumbled into her mind, foremost of which was anger. She had been right—all this had, after all, been a clever way of getting her to trust him and relax with him, so that he could make his move. And she thought she knew, too, exactly why he had decided to do it. He had met a girl who did not fall at his feet within seconds, and she had intrigued him, and so he had decided to take what he saw as the bait and change her attitude by hook or by crook. His pride couldn't take rejection . . .

He was still looking at her, waiting for an answer to his question. Cassie took a deep breath and replied levelly, 'I'd turn around and walk out of this room.'

'Would you?'

God, she thought, *can't he get a plain and simple message?*

'Yes, I would.'

'Why?'

He had moved closer to her, his hand hovering an

84

inch from her arm, and the dark-fringed grey eyes were alight. Suddenly something inside Cassie snapped. Stepping back, she said sharply, 'Because, Guy Carver, I'm not one of those women who's taken in by a handsome face and smooth words! If you want to make a conquest, go and find someone else! You may be a film star, and you may have girls trailing after you wherever you go and waiting for the chance to jump into bed with you, but I'm not one of them!'

The expression in Guy's eyes hardened, until they glittered like flint. 'How righteous of you! Saving yourself for Mr. Right are we?'

His immediate reaction had been to hit back, but it only served to make Cassie angrier. 'No, I'm not,' she retorted. 'But that doesn't mean I have to have my kicks with every conceited gigolo who thinks he's God's gift to women!' She was almost shouting now; the fury in her was rising like a tide. 'I thought when I came up here that you really were capable of being friendly and pleasant for its own sake, and not for what you could get out of it, but I was obviously wrong! I feel sorry for you!'

He raised his eyebrows, and his face was icily cold and contemptuous. 'Save your pity,' he told her savagely. 'It's a lot better, I assure you, than being a professional refrigerator!' He walked away from the window, across the room, then swung on his heel to face her again. 'Don't worry, I won't make the same mistake twice! Next time I feel like a pleasant evening, I'll find someone who behaves like a flesh-and-blood human being!'

Fuming, Cassie shouted back, 'I wouldn't advise it! You might find that real human beings can't be switched off like robots when you don't want to play with them any more!' She thumped her wine glass down so hard that its contents slopped over on to the table. 'Thanks for the drink!' And with that she pushed past him and strode out of the room, slamming the door with an echoing crash behind her.

7

Cassie slammed the door of her own room with an equally loud bang and threw herself on the bed, aware that she was shaking from head to foot with rage.

But was it rage? As she collected her wits and sat up, she was beginning to wonder. What, precisely, had made her fly off the handle so suddenly when Guy tried to make a pass at her? There had been nothing insulting about it really—he had merely asked her a question which had made it plain that he was interested in her. Any other girl would have been delighted. So why had she reacted so violently?

Her hands were still trembling, and picking up the telephone she dialled room service, and ordered a pot of coffee to be sent to her room, and then as she waited she tried to sort out her thoughts.

She had over-reacted, there was no doubt of that, and it disturbed her. Not that Guy wasn't to blame— it had been arrogant of him to assume that he could win her over so easily with a bottle of wine, a bit of Bach—he was probably used to bowling any woman over with a lot less effort. But on the surface there was no need for her to have reacted as strongly as she did. After all, she had half expected it, knowing his reputation, and so had been prepared for the worst. So why the explosion?

She had a horrible feeling that she knew the answer to that—she was frightened. Not of Guy himself, but of something vaguer, deeper rooted. If she was strictly honest with herself—and that was very hard indeed right now—she had to admit that despite her determination to dislike him, she did find Guy Carver very attractive. It was inevitable really; he had a face and a physique that most girls dreamed about, herself included, and when he wanted to turn on the charm he could be sweetness itself. But it wasn't that that had drawn her thoughts unwillingly in his direction; it was more his aura, that sense of something else hidden under the public mask.

She had appealed to his instinct for a challenge—well, he appealed to her own in the same way. She wanted to believe that he wasn't truly as conceited and arrogant as he made out; that under the surface was a very different and far more likeable personality which he kept hidden. And that, she knew, was a very dangerous line of thought to pursue. She had been aware of it when they stood together at the window; and when he had asked what she would do if he kissed her, well . . . she had known the real answer to that, as well. At that moment a part of her had wanted him to, and so her other side, her logical, practical side, had reacted by violently rejecting him and being very indignant about it. Not that he hadn't asked to be smacked in the face—he had a hell of a nerve if he thought he was so irresistible that a couple of drinks would win her over . . .

'Oh, *hell!*' She said the words aloud as she realized that her mind was starting to go round in circles. First she was condemning him, then making excuses for him, then condemning him again. This was ridiculous.

She was about to stand up and go into the bathroom,

thinking that a shower might clear her head, when there was a light knock at the door. Expecting the coffee, Cassie called out, 'Come in!'

The door opened and Anna Loriot slipped into the room.

'Anna!' Cassie was astonished, but pleased. The Frenchwoman was wearing a long lounging-coat that must have cost her a fortune in Paris, and had removed all her carefully applied makeup, so that she now looked like a homely—if very wealthy—grandmother.

'This is a surprise,' Cassie added warmly. 'Come in, please.' Right now, she thought, Anna was the person she most wanted to see. If anyone could calm her down and help her put things in perspective, it was this wise and kindly woman.

'Chérie.' Anna closed the door and glided towards the bed. 'Are you all right?' Her eyes searched Cassie's face, and Cassie knew she could not hide anything. She sighed.

'Yes, I'm fine.'

Anna pursed her lips. '"Fine", she says. Chérie, it is not my business to pry, but I was in my room— oh, those reporters, they have quite exhausted me with their questions!—and my room is next to Guy's.' Steadily she looked at Cassie, daring her to tell a lie. 'I heard an argument, a terrible argument. It was you, was it not?'

Cassie sank down on the bed. 'Yes, Anna, it was me.'

The Frenchwoman sat down beside her, and she caught a whiff of expensive perfume. A small, birdlike hand took hers in a firm grasp. 'What was it, chérie? Come, tell Anna. When a woman and a man quarrel, the woman needs to talk, to—how do you say—get it out of her system, yes? Brooding is bad for the complexion—it taints the blood and unbalances the health. Tell me, now.'

At that moment there was another tap at the door, and a waiter entered with a tray. 'You ordered coffee, madam?' he asked Cassie.

'Oh, yes—thank you.' Cassie hesitated. 'Do you think I could have another cup?'

'Of course, madam.' The waiter glided out, returned an astonishingly short time later, then at last Cassie and Anna were left alone.

Anna saw that Cassie's hands were still not quite steady, and poured the coffee herself. Sugaring Cassie's generously (it was, she said, good for calming the nerves) she settled back and said in a tone that would not take no for an answer, 'Now.'

The story came out. Cassie told her how Guy had been seeking her out all week for no apparent reason, and how she had agreed to go to his room for a drink, and finally of what had happened once she got there.

'I was just so *angry,*' she finished. 'It was the way he presumed that I would be as easy to persuade as all the other women he's had in his life.'

Anna shook her head and gave Cassie a sad smile. 'Why should he not?' she asked. 'After all, he does not know you as a person. To him, you are just another girl in the film business, you see? He is used to that type.' She sighed, pouring herself more coffee. 'You should not let him upset you, my dear. I am sure he meant no insult.' She hesitated, then, 'Perhaps you could try—though I know it is not easy—to make the allowance for him.'

'Allowance?' Cassie was taken aback. 'What do you mean?'

'Well... Guy is perhaps not all he seems.'

'I'm sorry, Anna, I don't understand.' Cassie was bewildered, but the Frenchwoman reached out and patted her arm.

'No. Of course. You do not know all. But there is a little story behind all of this, you understand? Not a pleasant story.'

Cassie leaned forward, intrigued. 'What is it, Anna? Please tell me.'

'It was all a long time ago,' Anna said. 'Ten years—Guy was very young, his career had just begun and he was almost unknown. He was married then—'

'Married?' Cassie was surprised. 'I didn't know that!'

'Few people do, my dear. But at the time I was working on a film in which Guy had a very small part. And so I witnessed all that happened, you see.'

'Go on.' Cassie's coffee was getting cold, but she didn't notice.

'Well, there was a very unpleasant scene. Guy's wife—a terrible girl, flighty, no good for him—she decided that he was not good enough for her. He was struggling to make ends meet, and she thought that he would never become famous—and fame was what she wanted. So she started to look around for a man who had more glamorous things to offer her.' Anna's lips pursed. 'It was not difficult for her. Whatever else she may have been, she was beautiful. Anyway, she attracted the attention of the director. They had an affair, and she made no attempt to hide it—in fact she flaunted it in poor Guy's face. Oh, she was very clever. The director was rich and successful; she wanted to be rid of her husband and marry him instead.

91

So she took Guy to court, claiming that he had been cruel to her—beating her, abusing her; she made up such a story!'

'And it wasn't true?'

Anna gave her a sidelong look. '*Chérie,* whatever you may think of Guy, he is not a monster! He loved that girl. He would have given her anything; but she—she could not wait. She would not stand by him, and all she wanted was to be free of him; she did not care how. She won her case—how I do not know; she must have bribed others to say the things they did about Guy—and when the case was over she was even granted alimony. A great deal of alimoney, more almost than Guy could pay.'

'And—the director?' Cassie asked.

'Oh, they did not marry. She lived with him for two years, I believe, while Guy continued to pay her money. But then she grew tired of him too. Now, I think, she is married to a very rich businessman and she lives in Greece.' Anna helped herself to a third cup of coffee, then continued, 'But now, perhaps, you will understand a little of why Guy is the way he is. The experience with his wife shattered him and it changed him. To stand up to such pain and such heartbreak, he had to become as hard as a rock, without room for the emotions, you see? She made him think that women are not to be trusted, that they are only out for what they can get, and now that feeling is embedded deep in his mind. He treats other girls as his wife once treated him, for he feels that that is the only way he can avoid being hurt again. Oh, he knows that they want him for his looks and his fame. And so he plays their game—and he wins every time.'

Cassie was silent for a while. Certainly what Anna had said did explain a great deal. But even so, she reasoned, Guy must surely have realized that she was not yet another girl who was going to chase him and get what she could from him. She had made that clear from the start.a So why had he gone to such lengths to try and seduce her?

The Frenchwoman spoke again, startling her. 'You are thinking, *chérie*, that that is still no excuse for his behaviour, yes?'

'Well...' Cassie pinkened and smiled, secretly thinking that Anna must have read her mind. 'Something like that, yes.'

'Ah, do not judge too harshly! I do not know for sure, but perhaps he thinks that you are playing the same game in a different way. Or maybe it is that he genuinely likes you!'

'If he does, he's got a strange way of showing it,' Cassie pointed out. 'But Anna, you seem to know him very well. If he told you about all this—well, he must trust someone.'

Anna chuckled softly. *'Chérie*, I am easy to trust where Guy is concerned. We have been friends a long time, though we meet rarely. And you see, there is no possibility that I could want what all these other women want from him, for I am almost old enough to be his grandmother!' When Cassie started to protest that she wasn't anything of the kind, Anna swept her words aside. 'No, no, don't pay me the compliments that I do not deserve! I am old and I do not mind admitting it. But sometimes the young find the old easier to trust, for there is no rivalry between them, and so it is less complicated.'

'You're right. And Anna, now that you've told me this story, I *do* feel sorry for Guy. But—'

'But it does not make you like him for what he did tonight? Of course not. I am not trying to matchmake between you. But if you understand a little, life might be easier while we are working, am I not right? Now, you are calmer? Good. I have achieved that, at least. And now I shall leave you in peace, for if I do not sleep soon I shall be a hag in the morning.' She rose. 'Sweet dreams, *chérie*. Au revoir.'

Anna was half way to the door before something jumped into place in Cassie's mind and clicked. It must have been what Anna had said about the young trusting the old.

'Anna...'

'What is it?' The Frenchwoman turned.

'I—maybe I should have said this before, but there is something else.'

'About Guy?'

'No. Well, not exactly, though I think he might be involved.'

It was on the tip of Anna's tongue to suggest that Cassie might wait till morning, but seeing her face the Frenchwoman realized that this was something very serious. She came back and sat down again. 'What is it?'

Cassie took a deep breath. 'I'm not sure yet, and I might be horribly wrong, but—it's about Van Hamer and Andrew Symes. I think there's something odd going on.'

Anna's eyes narrowed and she frowned. *'Odd?'* she said darkly.

'Something I overheard...Look, I'd better start from the beginning.' And Cassie told Anna all that had happened since she had eavesdropped on the conversation between Hamer and Symes on the night of the party. She recounted her visit to Hamer's office and the letters she had glimpsed, then reminded Anna of the strange question the reporter had asked about royalties at the press conference that very evening. When she finished her story, Anna got slowly to her feet.

'*Chérie*, I think you have stumbled upon something that Van Hamer would not like any of us to know. That man . . . I never trusted him, and as for Symes— he is a greedy little creature who would sell his own soul if the price was right.'

'You don't think I'm imagining things, then?' Cassie asked anxiously.

'Imagining? No. I do not. Tell me, have you said anything to Alan about this?'

'Not yet. I've been trying to find an opportunity, but he's always too busy. I was going to talk to him tonight.'

Immediately, Anna shook her head. 'Say nothing to him, please. Not yet. I am in a better position than you to make some discreet enquiries, and I think that I should do so before we take this any further. Softly softly catch the monkey—is that not what you say in English?'

'That's about it.' Cassie hid a smile; the phrase sounded comical in Anna's heavy French accent.

'Well, if these monkeys are playing tricks, you can be sure they will be on their guard and they will be hard to catch. Will you let me do what I can before you speak to Alan?'

Cassie wasn't entirely happy about that idea; after all, the sooner something was done, the more likely they would be to catch Hamer and Symes out before it was too late. But after all, there was little Alan could do even if he did know. Trying not to let the reluctance show in her voice, she said, 'All right, I'll agree to that. But there may not be much time.'

'Don't worry, *chérie*, I shall be as quick and as secret as the cat. I will find out what I can, see if there are more clues to be had, then we shall talk again. Perhaps tomorrow. And meanwhile do not worry. It is bad for the face—makes lines where there should be none! Good night, my dear.'

'Good night.' Cassie watched until the door closed behind Anna, then lay back on the bed.

'Damn!' she said aloud. It wasn't directed at anything in particular. But it made her feel better.

Cassie was dreading the following day on the film set. After last night's fracas, she wasn't sure if she could face meeting Guy. But when the star arrived in his Aston-Martin (he always drove himself, saying that he wouldn't trust any chauffeur to handle his beloved car) things weren't as bad as Cassie had feared. He merely nodded formally, gave her a cool 'Good morning' and said no more. Witnessing this chilly greeting Alan raised an eyebrow, but was too tactful to ask any questions. If Cassie and Guy had quarrelled about something, it wasn't his business, providing it didn't interfere with work.

However, as the day went on Cassie found herself watching Guy more closely than ever before. She was still angry with him, but after the story Anna had told her she was on the lookout for any telltale signs. And she found them. Today's scene had a lot of pathos, and although she knew that Guy was more than capable of playing the part convincingly, she thought she detected something genuine beneath his acting—a kind of extra sense of conviction, as if he knew only too well what his fictional self was feeling. She tried to tell herself, for self-defence's sake, that it was only a front, that she was falling for the trick of a good actor, but she couldn't make herself believe it. And when the cast broke off for lunch, Guy went off on his own, and she glimpsed him a few minutes later, sitting in a solitary chair with an odd, faraway look on his face that wasn't entirely happy. Even as she watched, someone approached him, and instantly that vulnerable look was masked, replaced by the quick, hard professional image.

Cassie wandered away, thoughtful. She was beginning to realize that her anger wasn't directed at Guy so much as at herself, and she knew why. Last night she had been unable to sleep; she had lain in bed tossing and turning, blaming her restlessness on everything from too many blankets to the city lights filtering in at the window, and refusing to admit the real cause.

She had been thinking about Guy. Something about him had been preying on her mind, upsetting her, to the point where she almost felt guilty about her own behaviour the previous evening. She couldn't put a finger on exactly what the problem was, but it worried her. It seemed to have some sort of power to hold her and trouble her, and she was afraid of it without knowing why.

'Cassie!' Alan's voice broke in on her reverie, and she turned to see him hurrying towards her. He grinned boyishly, and she knew by his look that he was about to ask a favour of her.

'Cass, I'm sorry to interrupt your lunch break,' he began, 'but I've just realized that I've left my full copy of the shooting script back at the hotel, and I want to check on some continuity. Would you be an angel and...'

'Go back and get it,' Cassie finished the sentence for him. 'Okay, boss-man, to hear is to obey. Is there a car I can take?' She was secretly relieved to have something to do that would take her mind off its present preoccupation, but it wouldn't do to admit that to Alan or she would never hear the end of it.

Alan ruffled her hair affectionately. 'Good for you! You can take the Mini that's parked over there—the keys are inside. Thanks, Cass!'

'My pleasure.' And as she walked off towards the car, Cassie was glad to be getting away from the set.

That evening, Cassie had not been in the hotel half an hour before a message was sent to her asking her to meet Anna Loriot in the Terrace Bar. Anna had not been on the set that day, as she was not needed. Making her way to the bar, Cassie wondered what it was that Anna had to tell her.

She soon found out. The Frenchwoman was sitting alone at a table by the big window and she had already ordered Cassie a stiff drink.

'Chérie—sit down.' Her voice was husky, as though she was afraid of being overheard, and she sounded excited. Smiling, Cassie thought that Anna was thoroughly enjoying being in the centre of a mystery, and she took a chair opposite her.

Anna leaned forward like a conspirator, her eyes sparkling. 'Chérie, I think you were right to be suspicious. I have been making enquiries here and there, and I can tell you now, there is something strange about the contracts we have all signed with Van Hamer's company!'

Cassie felt her pulse racing. 'What is it?' she asked eagerly.

Anna shook her head. 'As yet, I cannot be sure. But—you know that Van is only one of the company's directors?'

'Yes, I noticed that on their headed paper. But he is the top man, isn't he?'

'He and one other. But he has the power to sign the cheques, to make the decisions, to arrange things. That means that there is much he could do without the other directors having to know.'

'What are you getting at, Anna?'

'Just this. It could be—and I only say could—that Van has plans to, shall we say, make a little extra on the side for himself and for his friend Symes. How easy it would be, would it not, for him to arrange that there should be a little difference between the money his company agrees to pay to me, to Alan and to Guy, and the money that we all *think* we are to receive?'

'Ohh,' Cassie said. 'I begin to see the light...'

'Of course you do. And where would that difference go?'

'Into the pockets of those two crooks.'

'Precisely. And who would know the truth? No one. Mind you, I am not saying that this is true. But with all you have told me—the questions at the press conference—and from what I have found today, which would seem to point in the direction of something not right, I believe that is what they are doing, or something like it.'

Cassie sat back, biting her lip. 'But we still can't be certain.'

'No. You are right. What we need is evidence, hard evidence. The letters.'

'But how?'

Anna gave her a sidelong look. 'Well, *chérie*, I think that that must be up to you.'

'Me...?'

'You have been to the offices before. You must go

there again, at a time when Van is known to be away, and take copies of as many of the letters as you can. We cannot take the originals, for their disappearance would be noticed, and that would alert our friends. But we *must* have copies.'

She was right, though Cassie didn't relish the idea of making another trip to Soho after her narrow escape last time. But Anna did not know about that, and anyway she was right; Cassie was in the best position to get the letters.

'All right,' she said. 'I'll try. Hamer's supposed to be spending some time on the set next week to see what Alan's doing with his money, so I should have a chance.'

'Bravo, *chérie!* And now, I shall leave you.' Anna's eyes twinkled wickedly. 'Tonight I have the facial mask and an early night. Tomorrow we do not work, and I am to meet an old flame. We shall wine and dine together, and I shall feel young again. There is no better tonic, yes?'

'Yes,' Cassie agreed, laughing, and they both rose to leave the bar.

'And as for the letters,' Anna added, 'I shall cross the fingers.'

Yes, Cassie thought fervently, *you do that! I'm going to need all the help I can get . . .*

8

Cassie's chance came sooner than she could have hoped. The following evening Alan came into the hotel restaurant with a long face, and when he sat down he announced that he had just had a call from Van Hamer.

'He wants to come down and watch the filming tomorrow,' he complained. 'And of course I couldn't say no, could I? That's all I need—a busybody producer breathing down my neck all day!'

'He'll probably get bored and go away after a couple of hours,' Cassie told him soothingly, and then, remembering her plan, asked, 'What time is he arriving?'

'About ten.' Alan sighed. 'Yes, you're probably right, Cass. And I suppose he had to come some time, and this'll get at least one visit out of the way. Warn everyone to be on their best behaviour, will you?'

'Will do.' She wasn't really concentrating on what he said. Ten o'clock—it should be easy to find an excuse to slip away from the set just before he arrived, and then...

She was on tenterhooks from the moment she got out of bed on the following day, but if Alan noticed her nervousness he didn't comment on it. Everything went smoothly, and by nine-thirty Cassie was about ready to leave. She had managed to avoid being given any errands to run, and at a quarter to ten she asked the continuity girl to tell Alan that she had gone back to the hotel for something and that she would return soon. The Mini—one of two which were always available for anyone who needed them—was parked in its usual place, and Cassie drove away from the set.

She was in Soho by ten-fifteen, and managed to find a parking meter. She had carefully worked out her plan, and hoped that it would sound plausible to Hamer's staff.

She was relieved to see, when she walked into the building, that a different receptionist sat at the desk. Encouraged, Cassie marched up to her.

'Hello. Is Mr. Hamer in?'

'No.' The girl looked up; she seemed half-asleep. 'He's down at a film set.'

'Oh, well, I'm Alan Blythe's assistant—he's the director on the film. Alan wanted something photocopied, and I wondered if I could use your machine here?'

'Yes, of course. The only thing is, Mr. Hamer's secretary isn't in yet.'

'Well, I know my way up to the offices. If that would be all right. I would wait, but these are needed urgently.' She brandished a sheaf of papers.

The receptionist hesitated, then: 'Yes, I'm sure no one would mind. The copier's in the secretary's office. Do you know where that is?'

'Yes, thanks. I won't be long.' And Cassie ran for the stairs.

So far, she had had incredibly good luck. She would have the photocopier and the office to herself—which meant that she could easily sneak the relevant letters out of the file and put them back afterwards without anyone being the wiser. She let herself into the office and found the photocopier under the window. Now, the files...

It was difficult to decide which letters were the important ones, so Cassie planned to take out anything that referred to Alan, Guy or Anna from that file and copy it anyway. Aware that the secretary could interrupt her at any moment, she decided to remove the letters two at a time, so that they would be easier to hide under her bogus file if anyone came in.

Looking for something of real importance, she struck gold almost immediately. It was a letter from Andrew Symes to Van Hamer, and it was the most damning piece of evidence she had yet found. One paragraph was what really gave it away:

'The arrangements you suggested suit me ideally, and the split between us is agreed. There is no possibility that Guy Carver could find out; he has no access to my files, and I've made quite sure that Anna Loriot's agent will not get wind of this. In my opinion, Van, they are all receiving enough money to keep them happy anyway. They accepted the contract as we "revised" it, and there's no way that any of them can find out that the company are actually paying out a great deal more, as they have no contact with the other directors. And what they don't know can't hurt them...'

The tone of the letter was triumphant, almost crowing, and Cassie thought that Van Hamer was either supremely confident or supremely stupid to leave these in an office file. No doubt Symes had taken greater precautions and his copies were locked in a safe somewhere. But with this, she had the evidence she needed. Anna would be delighted.

She switched on the photocopier and ran the letter through it. Slipping the copy into her own file she picked up the second of the two letters she had chosen to begin with. And the copy was just sliding out of the machine when the door opened.

A pert, small girl with short dark hair came in. She paused when she saw Cassie, then smiled and said brightly, 'Hello. You must be Alan Blythe's assistant. How are you getting along? Need any help?'

Cassie's heart sank. Here she was, with only two letters copied safely, when she had hoped for at least another ten minutes alone. She forced a smile in answer.

'No, I'm fine thanks. Nearly finished.' This was going to be difficult—somehow she had to get the two originals back into the file without arousing any suspicions. And as for the rest of the letters—well, she would have to make do with what she had, and hope that it was enough.

Hamer's secretary hung up her jacket and started to busy herself at her desk. Cassie hastily took one of the unimportant papers from her own file and, for appearance's sake, ran it through the machine. 'Nearly done,' she said, unnecessarily. The secretary wasn't listening. She had pulled out her audio machine and was running through a tape of letters that her boss had left to be typed. *Maybe,* Cassie thought, *while she's occupied I can just slip the letters back*.

She opened the drawer of the filing cabinet, then glanced up. The secretary took no notice. And why should she? Cassie reasoned suddenly. After all, she had no reason to think that anything odd was going on. Suddenly more confident, she put the letters back in their places, then gathered up her file, together with the two precious copies, and moved towards the door.

'That's the lot,' she said cheerfully. 'I'll leave you in peace. Thanks very much.'

And with that, she left the office and hurried back to the car.

Cassie drove back to the film set feeling both elated and disappointed. She was disappointed that she had not had time to copy more letters, yet elated in that the ones she *did* have would be very valuable indeed. But when she reached the set, the letters went out of her mind in an instant.

She was just turning into the area where the crew were working when she heard the sound of an ambulance siren, and seconds later the vehicle came tearing round the corner in the opposite direction, from the filming site. It disappeared with squealing tyres, and Cassie's heart missed a beat. Had there been an accident on the set? Who was hurt? White-faced, she stamped on the Mini's accelerator and hurtled round the corner to screech to a halt near one of the big cameras.

She was confronted with chaos, and in the middle of the chaos was Alan, who was waving his arms around and looking generally very agitated. Cassie's first thought was one of relief that he at least was all right—and Guy was standing a few yards away, so it wasn't him either. Who, then ... ?

She ran up to Alan. 'Alan! What's been happening?'

He swung round, and looked thankful to see her. 'Cass! Where the hell have you been?' And without waiting for an explanation he went on, 'We're in a complete stew here—Anna's collapsed.'

'*Collapsed?*' Cassie was horrified. 'Whatever happened?'

'We don't know. One minute she said she was feeling a bit queasy, the next she was on the floor. The ambulance men reckoned it was food poisoning.'

'Oh, my God!' Cassie said, horrified.

'Don't worry,' Alan told her sourly. 'She'll be all right once they get her to hospital. No danger or anything. But this is going to play merry hell with our schedules!'

Not only the schedules, Cassie thought. Poor Anna.

'All because she went out with some damned gigolo yesterday and lived it up!' Alan said explosively. 'Now, where's Van Hamer? I've got to sort this out. Hell's bells!' And he stamped off across the set to where Van Hamer was talking to the assistant director.

Cassie thought that it would be as well to keep out of his way until he had simmered down. Certainly this was not the time to tackle him about the letters: that would have to wait. Probably the day's filming would now be called off, so when she got back to the hotel she would find out which hospital Anna was in and telephone to find out how soon she could see her. Failing that, she had no idea what to do for the best.

Within an hour, the disconsolate cast were back at the Albury Hotel. Alan and Hamer immediately locked themselves away in Hamer's suite for a discussion, and Cassie managed to find out where Anna had been taken. She rang the hospital, and enquired after Miss Loriot. The receptionist was very helpful. Yes, Miss Loriot had been brought in; was Cassie a relative?

'No,' Cassie said, 'I'm the personal assistant to Alan Blythe, the director of the film Miss Loriot was working on when she collapsed. We're all very worried about her, and of course we also need to know how long she's likely to be in hospital.'

The receptionist made enquiries and came back to her. She told her that Anna did have food poisoning, but that it was not too serious and she would recover. However, she could have no visitors for at least a few days.

Cassie cursed under her breath, but there was nothing she could do. She asked the receptionist to pass on everyone's good wishes, and said that she would be in touch again soon for a progress report. She put the phone down, and turned to see Guy Carver standing beside her.

She was in a public booth in the hotel lobby, and from the expression on Guy's face she guessed that he had overheard most of the conversation.

'Is she going to be all right?' he asked. He sounded very worried; there was no trace of the uneasy coolness that had existed between them since the disastrous evening in his suite.

Cassie nodded, slumping back against the wall. 'Yes, she'll be okay. It is food poisoning. They say she can't have any visitors for a few days.'

'I'm not surprised. But that seems to bother you.'

Cassie gave him a long, searching look. With no possibility that she could see Anna, and with Alan in no fit state to be told about the letters, there was only one other person to whom she could show her evidence—Guy himself. He was involved, after all. And she had the feeling that this just couldn't wait any longer.

'Yes, it does bother me,' she said. 'And for a very good reason. Guy, have you got a few minutes to spare?'

She thought he looked wary, but he said, 'Yes. What's the problem?'

'There's something you ought to know about. Let's

107

go and get some coffee, and I'll tell you all about it.'

They went into one of the hotel lounges, and when coffee came and she had checked that neither Van Hamer nor Symes was anywhere around, Cassie took the copied letters from her bag and laid them on the table in front of Guy. 'Read those.'

Guy read them, then looked up. His face was tight and his eyes shocked. 'Where did you find these?'

'In a file in Hamer's office. Listen, I'll tell you the whole story.' And she repeated the tale as she had told it to Anna. Guy listened without interrupting, but a frown creased his brow that grew deeper as Cassie talked. When she finished she looked at the letters again.

'So it looks like you've uncovered a neat little plan to cheat us out of a great deal of money. God almighty! Those slimy . . .' he shook his head. 'Does anyone else know about this?'

'Only Anna. I told her the other night, and she's been making some enquiries too. In fact I was going to show her these letters before she went into hospital, but there was no time. I haven't told Alan yet, because he's been too busy.'

'Yes,' Guy said grimly, ''and now he's going to be even less likely to have any time to listen. But we can't just sit back and do nothing. We'll have to . . .'

He was interrupted at that moment by a discreet voice on the Tannoy system. 'Paging Mr. Guy Carver. Paging Mr. Guy Carver.'

'Damn!' Guy said. 'I'd better see who wants me. Wait here; I'll be back in a moment.' He hurried away, and Cassie put the letters back into her bag. It was an inexpressible relief to have shown the letters to someone else, and she was glad that Guy had been so willing to take her seriously.

Guy was back, as promised, moments later. He looked harassed. 'I've got to go,' he told her. 'Alan and Hamer are reorganizing the filming schedule to allow for Anna, and they need me to help finalize it. It shouldn't take too long—but I must see you afterwards.'

'I'll be around here somewhere,' Cassie promised.

'I'll find you. And don't worry—I won't try to say anything to Alan, not under Hamer's nose. See you later.' And he went, crossing the foyer with his long-legged stride.

Cassie killed time for an hour, first trying to concentrate on reading a newspaper, then just wandering round the lobby and watching the people who came in and out of the hotel. She kept a weather eye on the lifts, and breathed a sigh of thankfulness when at last a lift door slid open and Guy stepped out.

He saw her immediately and came over. Taking her arm in a firm grip, he led her back towards the coffee lounge.

They sat down, and Guy leaned forward. 'It's all been decided,' he said. 'They've managed to rearrange everything and they're going to do some minor scenes over the next few days. I won't be needed at least until Wednesday, so I'm going to take a trip home.'

'Home?' Cassie asked.

'Sussex.' He smiled wryly, remembering his secrecy the last time she had asked him where he lived.

'If it's all right with you, I think these letters ought to go straight to a solicitor. My usual lawyer here in London also does business for Andrew Symes, so there's no question of using him. But I've got a friend in the village where I live, a local guy, and I know

I can trust him—he's a good solicitor. The thing is, Cassie—could you come with me?'

Cassie's look became wary. After all the tension between them, she was not sure that a journey to Sussex with him would be such a good idea. 'Why?' she asked.

'You're the only person who can tell the full story at first hand. And if we're going to clear this up and catch Hamer and Symes at it, you're going to be needed. I'm sure Alan would give you the rest of the day off, and it's still early—we could get there easily by mid-afternoon. Please, Cassie—if not for my sake, then for Alan's.'

He had hit her where she was most vulnerable, and reluctantly she nodded. 'All right. I'd better leave a message for him, as he might be with Hamer for ages yet. He'll want to kill me when he finds out I've just disappeared, but it's all in a good cause.'

Guy looked relieved. 'Right. How quickly can you be ready?'

'Give me five minutes.'

'I'll meet you here.'

Cassie went to her room, and as the lift carried her upwards she told herself firmly that it was *only* for Alan's sake that she had agreed to go with Guy. But she had to admit that she was looking forward to seeing his home. With a smile she realized that she was highly privileged; from what she could gather, it was hallowed ground and hardly anyone was ever allowed to invade it. She only hoped that no more rows flared up between herself and Guy; she would have to be on her best behaviour, and hope that he would be too. And once they had seen this solicitor friend, they could be back in London almost before it was dark.

In her room, in a sudden rush of vanity, she retouched her makeup, telling herself that it was no more than human pride and that she had no particular wish to impress Guy. Then, slipping the cosmetics purse into her handbag and dousing herself with a liberal burst of cologne, she picked up a light jacket and went back downstairs. Guy was waiting, and Cassie left a message with reception to be passed on to Alan. Minutes later they were climbing into the sleek Aston-Martin and nosing out of the hotel's underground car park for the journey to Sussex.

9

Despite her misgivings, Cassie soon began to enjoy the drive. The Aston-Martin was the last word in luxury, and once they were out of the frustrating London traffic and heading south on the main Brighton road, Guy gave the powerful engine its head, and they sped through leafy countryside at a speed well above the legal limit.

Small talk would have been awkward for them both under the circumstances, and to Cassie's relief Guy put on a tape of relaxing music and concentrated on his driving, not speaking. It was a bright, sunny day, and Cassie was content just to watch the scenery gliding by. Again it astonished her how green England was, and once they reached the southern side of Surrey and the landscape began to change, she was doubly impressed. From woody ground dotted with towns that still had more than a touch of suburbia about them, the scene changed to rolling hills and downs, with at last the breathtaking view of what looked like towering inland cliffs in the distance.

'That's the Sussex Downs,' Guy said when she commented on them.

'They're beautiful! So peaceful...'

He gave her a sidelong look of warm approval. 'Yes. That's why I love living among them.'

'But why are they called downs when really they're ups?'

Guy laughed. 'Don't ask me! I've never thought about it. One of our English eccentricities, I suppose.' They whipped past a signpost and he added, 'Only another ten miles and we'll be there. I only hope Charles is in.

'Didn't you call him?'

'I tried, but the whole office was at lunch and I got a recorded message. That's the thing about country places—absolutely everything stops for lunch. Anyway, he's sure to be back sometime. Why, are you worried about the time we get back?' There was a gently teasing note in his voice, and Cassie reddened. Turning away so that he wouldn't see her colour, she said lamely,

'Well . . . Alan's going to slaughter me if I'm too late.'

'He ought to give you a medal when he finds out why you've been away,' Guy pointed out, then added seemingly as an afterthought, 'You're not scared of him, are you?'

'Of course I'm not!' Cassie retorted hotly. 'Alan's not like that!'

Guy gave her a long look. 'I'm sure he's not. So why should he get upset?' When she didn't answer he said, 'Anyway, this needn't take long, and I'll drive you straight back to London if you're so worried about what dear Alan's going to say.'

There was a sharp silence. The last thing Cassie had wanted was to trigger Guy off into one of his sarcastic moods, but it seemed she had succeeded in doing just that. She comforted herself with the thought that she had made her point about not wanting to stay in Sussex.

After a few minutes Guy said abruptly—and almost too casually—'How long have you been working for Alan?'

Cassie thought back and made a quick mental calculation. 'About three years,' she told him.

'Hmm.' That could have meant anything, she thought. He said nothing else for a minute or so, then asked her, 'How did you get the job? It must have been a real plum.'

For a moment it was on the tip of Cassie's tongue to retaliate angrily; the way he had phrased it, the question had sounded like an insult—a kind of 'How come an idiot like you managed to land a job like this?', but she checked the impulse, telling herself not to be so prickly. It was very unlikely that Guy had meant it in any derogatory way: and even if she had any reason for being suspicious she ought to give him the benefit of the doubt.

She leaned further back in her seat. 'It was purely the luck of the draw, I suppose. I've always been fascinated by the film world, and I used to read all the trade magazines in Australia. The job was advertised, I applied, and—presto! I got it.'

'Alan interviewed you himself, did he?'

'Yes,' she replied, then, curious, 'Why do you ask?'

Guy shrugged. 'Oh, I just wondered. Alan strikes me as the kind of guy who'd be very thorough about things like that.'

'Yes, he is.' She stared sideways at him, wondering what he was getting at. His mind was chewing something over—she could almost hear the wheels turning round in his head—but she wasn't sure what it was. Why should he be so curious about herself and Alan?

She would have liked to ask him outright what he meant by all these odd questions, but decided against it. If he knew she was curious, he'd probably clam up and refuse to say another word.

He was silent again for a short while, leaving her wondering what was going on in that enigmatic mind of his, and she became so preoccupied that when his voice broke into her thoughts she visibly jumped.

'You get on very well with Alan, don't you,' he said.

'Yes.'

'Not like the usual boss-assistant relationship.'

Cassie replied without thinking. 'God, no! Any of that "do this, Miss MacRae, do that, Miss MacRae" and I'd be off! I had enough of that sort of thing in my first job after I left school—I couldn't stand it. No; Alan's great—it's just like working with a big brother.'

Guy nodded non-committally, and a slight frown creased his forehead, making his grey eyes seem startlingly bright under the overhang of dark brows.

'So, I suppose when this is all over, you and big brother will jet off back to Australia.'

'Well, of course we will,' she told him, surprised by such a peculiar statement. 'That's where we live!'

He gave a short, almost humourless laugh. 'It sounds like something out of a fairy tale—"and they all lived happily ever after". Do you think you'll live happily ever after, Cassie?'

She turned in her seat to look fully at him. 'What a crazy question! How the hell am I supposed to know what I'll be doing in ten or twenty years' time?'

He shrugged, refusing to be stung by her irritable tone. 'Well, you've got it made really, haven't you?

115

I don't think it would take a clairvoyant to see your future.'

It suddenly dawned on Cassie just what he meant—what he had been hinting at and leading up to all this time. Guy was fishing—fishing for more information about her relationship with Alan. He had watched them together, seen the way they worked and the way they teased each other, and he had jumped to the conclusion that they were, to say the least, more than friends.

Suddenly she wanted to laugh. The idea of her and Alan carrying on some clandestine and passionate love affair outside their working hours was quite ludicrous—Alan was very definitely not Cassie's type, and vice versa. But on reflection she could see how any outsider could get the wrong impression from their behaviour. As Guy had said, theirs was certainly no ordinary boss-assistant relationship.

It occurred to her then that there was no apparent reason for Guy to give a damn either way about what she and Alan might or might not do in their spare time. He couldn't have any professional criticisms, that was for sure—so why was he so interested?

If the man beside her had been anyone other than Guy Carver, then the reason would have been obvious—jealousy. But from their first meeting she had had the distinct feeling that Guy would rather have jumped off the Post Office tower than fall in love with his director's assistant, and Cassie had spent many hours telling herself firmly that the feeling was mutual. The only possibility she could think of—and she guessed it was more than a possibility—was that Alan had put Guy's nose out of joint. He was so used to women who fawned on him and chased him, that he didn't like to come across one who put another man before him in her affections. Perhaps he wanted to reassure himself that Cassie and Alan's relationship *was* purely professional, so that he needn't suffer any blows to his ego.

For a moment she wondered if she was being uncharitable and misjudging Guy's motives. Surely he wasn't so petty as to take an attitude like that—whatever her opinion of him might be, she found that hard to believe. But there had to be some explanation for this sudden interest in her welfare. What had he said? *You've got it made really, haven't you?* He had sounded quite sad when he said it. Or had that been her imagination? Hard to say now.

'You've gone very quiet,' he said.

She looked away from him, out of the window. 'Yes, I was just...thinking.'

'About?' he prompted.

'Oh...about what you said just now. You're wrong, you know.'

'Am I?'

'Yes. I haven't got anything made.'

He laughed again, and this time there was an edge of bitterness which he tried to hide by putting a sarcastic hint into his voice. 'Pull the other leg, Cassie, it's got bells on! You're laughing, and you know it.'

Disliking his implications, Cassie replied sharply, 'Because of Alan?'

'You said it, not me.'

In that moment, Cassie decided that this had gone far enough. 'Look, Guy,' she said, her voice quiet but teetering on the edge of real anger, 'I don't want to start arguing with you, but I want to get one thing straight. You seem to think there's something going on between Alan and me—well, you can put that right out of your head! People like you seem to think that a woman and a man only have to smile at each other

117

and they're having an affair! Well, maybe that's true for you, but in Australia we're a bit less childish!' She paused for breath, expecting Guy to come back at her, but to her surprise he said nothing, only waited for her to go on. A little daunted by his lack of reaction she nonetheless continued, 'If it satisfies your curiosity, Alan and I are *not* having an affair, and we never will! I think you've got quite a lot to learn about what it means to be good friends with someone. So you can stop asking probing questions and just forget about it, okay?'

There was an awful silence, during which Cassie was only waiting for the storm to break. With Guy's temper, it wouldn't have surprised her if he'd stopped the car and thrown her out—or maybe not even bothered to stop it, but thrown her out anyway! So she was doubly astonished when at last he shrugged his shoulders and said mildly,

'Well, that's put me firmly in my place, hasn't it?'

Cassie reddened. His reaction made her feel that she had overdone it and been too harsh with him. Awkwardly, by now feeling horribly embarrassed, she said, 'I didn't mean—'

He interrupted her. 'Yes, you *did* mean, and you had every right to. I'm sorry. I was being inquisitive, and it's none of my business. I accept the rebuke.'

He was actually *smiling,* she realized, as if he was pleased by what she had said. Totally confused, she decided that the best thing to do was put an end to this conversation as quickly as possible. But before she did, she had to make quite sure that what she had said had really got through to him.

'Forget it,' she said. 'I suppose I shouldn't have flown off the handle the way I did. But I want to make quite sure that you haven't got the wrong idea, Guy.'

He grinned at her. 'Of course I haven't. You and Alan are just good friends!'

'Right. And we'll stay that way as long as he pays my salary!'

'So you're both footloose and fancy free.' He was starting to tease her, but it was a relief after the tension.

'That's it,' Cassie agreed.

'I'm glad to hear it.'

She glanced at him. 'Are you? Why?'

'Isn't it obvious?' Guy said with a laugh. 'If we get back to London late, I was having visions of being confronted by a mad director in a fit of jealousy! Now I know I'll only have Big Brother to contend with!'

Cassie bristled inwardly. That was typical of him—as if Alan could think for a moment that she would—oh, she told herself, let it drop. He was only joking, after all.

They fell silent, both glad of the chance to relax a little before they arrived in Guy's home village. But as the car purred on, Cassie was still wondering just what had prompted Guy to start probing about herself and Alan in the first place. She decided that it must have been no more than idle curiosity. It *was* unfair to think that it was a matter of satisfying his ego; he wasn't *that* bad. And as for the idea of his being jealous—no, she told herself, ignoring the twinge of regret that accompanied that thought. Not Guy Carver. Not in a million years.

Minutes later they turned off the main road. The car nosed through a narrow, winding lane, over a river bridge, and at last they arrived at their destination.

The village almost took Cassie's breath away. It was one of those places that summed up England at its most beautiful, and which she had always thought must be an invention of the guide books. Trees rose

behind the main street, which was lined with old buildings most of which had been turned into shops and
offices without losing any of their original charm. A
church dominated the scene, squat and mellow with
a tall spire, and Guy pulled up the Aston-Martin on
the pavement beside it.

'Charles's office is just across the road,' he said.
'Come on—let's see if he's back.'

His earlier good mood had returned in full, and
Cassie thought that he seemed, if anything, more
cheerful than ever. She was thankful that the incident
in the car had not left an unpleasant atmosphere between them, and was content to forget the whole thing
and act as though nothing had happened.

The church clock was striking three-thirty as they
climbed out of the car, and Cassie took a deep breath.
'The air even smells green!' she said in astonishment.

'It's a bit different from London, isn't it?' Guy said
amusedly.

'You're telling me! I can understand why you chose
it as a place to live.'

Guy's face closed then, and Cassie wondered if she
had said the wrong thing. But after a moment his
expression cleared, and he said, 'Come on. We've got
business to do, remember?'

They crossed the road, and walked up to a Regency-
looking house with a panelled oak door. Beside the
door was a brass plaque that read, 'Martin & Beresford, Solicitors and Commissioners for Oaths'. Guy
pushed the door open and ushered Cassie in.

It was a typical solicitor's office, painted in subdued
colours and furnished with restrained good taste. A
middle-aged receptionist asked politely if she could
help them, and Guy asked for Mr. Charles Martin.

'I'm sorry, sir,' the receptionist said, 'but Mr. Martin's out of the office at the moment. I don't know whether he'll be back this afternoon. Can I leave a message, or can Mr. Beresford help?'

'No, I wanted to see Charles. I'd better leave a message. Could you ask him to ring Guy Carver at home, as soon as he comes back please? It's very urgent.'

'Mr. Guy Carver, at home, very urgent.' The receptionist carefully wrote it down. Obviously Guy's name rang no bells and Cassie guessed that she must be one of those people who never went to the cinema and only read *Country Life*.

'Thank you,' Guy said, and they left the office.

Out in the street once more, Cassie said, 'Well, what do we do now?'

Guy sighed heavily. 'We'll have to go back to my house, wait there and hope that Charles rings. If he doesn't, I'll try and call him at home.' He glanced at her. 'Sorry about this.'

'It doesn't matter.' She smiled, to reassure herself as much as him.

'Okay, let's go back to the car. It's about half a mile to the house.'

The Aston-Martin purred out of the main centre of the village, and a couple of minutes later drew up outside a white-painted Georgian house that stood back from the road in a secluded place of its own. The house wasn't particularly large—Cassie guessed about four bedrooms—but it had an elegant air that made it look grander than it really was.

Guy stopped the car, got out and said, 'Welcome to my retreat.'

Half out of her seat, Cassie hesitated. 'Are you sure you don't mind?' she asked uneasily.

He smiled. 'I'm not that much of a hermit, and I

somehow don't think you'll print the address in tomorrow's papers. Come on in.'

Still a little uncertain, she followed him to the front door. A rambling rose, bursting with new buds, climbed up the front wall, and pots of geraniums flanked the porch.

Guy unlocked the front door and stood back to let her go inside.

As she stepped over the threshold, a door to one side of the hall opened and a middle-aged woman wearing a flowered apron came out. She stopped short when she saw Cassie, but then, glimpsing Guy behind her, her expression cleared.

'Mrs. Harrison.' Guy was smiling. 'I forgot that you'd be here this afternoon. I'm sorry, have we disturbed you?'

The woman smiled broadly. 'No, Mr. Carver, of course you haven't. But is something wrong? I thought you were in London?'

'This is just a flying visit. Oh, I'd like you to meet Cassie MacRae. Cassie, this is Mrs. Harrison. Without her, my house would fall to rack and ruin.' And he winked at Mrs. Harrison, who shook her head in mock disapproval.

'Pleased to meet you, miss.' She spoke formally, extending a hand, and as she took it Cassie could see surprise in the other woman's eyes. She was being assessed, she knew, and something in Mrs. Harrison's glance told her that for Guy to bring a girl to his home was a very rare occurrence indeed. For some reason that thought cheered her.

'Well, let's go into the sitting-room. Through there.' Guy ushered Cassie through a door, and Mrs.

Harrison said, 'Shall I make you some coffee before I go?'

'That would be very kind of you, but could we make it tea?' He turned to Cassie. "I'll bet you've never tasted a cup of expertly-made English tea in your life.'

The housekeeper went out, closing the door behind her, and Guy said, 'Well. This is home. What do you think of it?'

Cassie turned slowly full circle, taking in the room. It was large enough to be uncluttered but small enough to be cosy. Comfortable armchairs flanked the fireplace, and the carpet underfoot felt as thick and luxurious as fur. On the mantel and a small side table was an assortment of mementos ranging from repertory notices to acting awards. But she noticed immediately that there were no photographs; no family pictures such as might be expected in any comfortable home. It reminded her sharply of what Anna had said about Guy's past. Across the room, french windows opened on to a rather overgrown garden.

Still thinking about the photographs, Cassie faced Guy again. 'It's beautiful,' she said warmly. 'Really beautiful. I can see now why you stay in England, if you've got a place like this to come back to.'

Guy laughed. 'I've got Mrs H to thank for most of it,' he admitted. 'Without her, the place would look like a pigsty. Bachelors aren't the most tidy people. But she comes in twice a week and goes through it like a whirlwind.'

Cassie sat down in one of the chairs. 'I suppose I'm very privileged,' she said slowly, 'being invited into your home.'

Guy looked at her oddly for a moment, as if wondering whether she was trying to provoke him. But he must have given her the benefit of the doubt, for after a few seconds he smiled.

'Something like that. When we've had tea, I'll show you round.'

Mrs Harrison came in then with a tray on which were a cheerful china teapot, two cups and a plate of biscuits. Guy thanked her, and when she had gone they sat in silence for a while. There was no tension between them, almost for the first time, and Cassie felt more relaxed than she had ever done before with him. The incident of Saturday night seemed, thankfully, to have been forgotten, or at least tactfully ignored.

When the tea was drunk, Guy took her on the promised inspection tour, and for the next hour she was absorbed in looking over the house and garden. By the end of it, she had come to the conclusion that Guy had very good and surprisingly subtle taste; anyone who had seen only his public side would never guess that his home would be so unassuming and peaceful. At last they ended the tour back in the sitting-room and Guy glanced at his watch.

'Good grief, it's five-thirty! And Charles hasn't phoned...'

'Maybe he didn't get your message,' Cassie suggested.

'No, he'll have got it if he's there—the receptionist's very reliable. I'll just have to try him at home.' He crossed to the telephone, checked the number in a small, battered book and dialled. A pause, then:

'Janet? Hello, it's Guy... Yes, very well thank you, and you?... Good. Look, I'm sorry to bother you, but I've been trying to get in touch with Charles, and he's been out of the office all day... Yes, it is very urgent as a matter of fact... Oh, I see. Well, yes, I'll have to... Thanks very much. 'Bye.'

He put the receiver down and turned to Cassie. 'Damn!'

'What's the matter?'

'He's gone down to Southampton on business, and he won't be back until the small hours.'

'Oh.' Cassie's face fell. 'What do we do now?'

Guy hesitated. 'Well, there's only one thing we can do, as far as I can see. Neither of us *has* to be back tonight. Do you mind staying here until tomorrow?'

Cassie bridled inwardly at that, and it must have shown immediately on her face, for Guy gave a wry laugh.

'Don't worry, I mean separate bedrooms. God knows there's enough room here.' And with grim humour he added, 'It's all right, Cassie, this isn't all part of a careful plot! You don't honestly think I'd go to these lengths just to lure you into my clutches, do you?'

Cassie blushed. 'Well, when you said it out of the blue like that—'She began, but he interrupted her.

'I know, you didn't trust my motives. I owe you an apology over that, don't I?'

'Well...'

'I *am* sorry. It was a stupid thing to do the other night, and I can't blame you for reacting the way you did.'

She was glad to hear him say it; though he seemed slightly embarrassed, the apology was genuine enough, and she was willing—almost *too* willing said a small voice at the back of her mind—to accept it.

'Let's forget it and be friends, shall we?' she suggested.

Guy looked relieved. 'Then you don't mind staying?'

'I don't mind.' And suddenly Cassie realized that she was glad at the prospect of spending a night under this roof.

'Well,' Guy said, 'to make up for the inconvenience, I'm going to take you out to dinner tonight. There's a quiet restaurant near here that's very good. Suit you?'

'Lovely! Though I'm not dressed for it. . .'

'Oh, forget that. This is the country, remember? No one dresses up round here. I'll phone the restaurant now and book a table.'

And so at eight o'clock they walked into the dimly-lit Golden Lion. Like the village in which it stood, the restaurant was gloriously Old English—all polished wood, dark leather and gleaming copper.

Guy had changed into dark trousers and a soft green shirt, with a dark cravat tied loosely at his throat. Once they had sat down and made themselves comfortable, Cassie was able to take a long and thoughtful look at him. Maybe it was the lighting, but the harsh edge seemed to have gone from his face, the sharp cheekbones softened, the grey eyes calmer and quieter. For the first time, she thought, she was seeing him in his true element; not the hurly-burly of the London social whirl, but the gentler pace of the country. Here there was no one to trouble him, no flocks of girls all vying for his attention, no meaningless flattery, no competition. This was the real Guy Carver. And she liked it.

They ordered, and Guy chose a light wine to drink with the meal. It was quite strong, and by the time Cassie finished the last forkful of her succulent steak, she was beginning to feel light-headed. The wine had also had its effect on Guy; he had relaxed, and his conversation had become more animated as the meal progressed. After a dessert, he ordered a brandy for them both, and when it came he leaned back in his chair and gave her a long, assessing look.

'You look lovely,' he said at last.

Cassie glanced down at her clothes and laughed self-consciously. 'I don't, and you know it.'

'Yes you do. It takes more than clothes to make a beautiful woman, you know. You look natural, Cassie, totally natural, and that's a rare thing. So many girls . . . well, they dress up like birds of paradise, and they think that's the best way to impress people, but they're wrong. No amount of decoration can compare with what you are.'

'And what's that?' she asked, her voice serious.

'You're genuine. A real person. There aren't many of them left.'

For a fleeting moment Cassie wondered if he was drunk, but he wasn't. The wine was simply loosening his tongue, and she was witnessing him now at his most honest—and perhaps also at his most vulnerable. One long finger was tapping restlessly on the stem of his glass, and he glanced round the restaurant as if wanting to make sure they were not overheard before he spoke again.

At last he said, 'I sometimes wish I'd chosen another business to be in.'

Cassie didn't comment; it would have been foolish to ask why, as she already knew the answer. 'You don't have to get involved any more than you want to,' she said gently.

'Don't I?' Guy looked cynical. 'I'm not big enough to shut myself away and do what Anna's done—I'd be forgotten in six months. But I'm getting to hate the phoniness of it all—the girls in particular.'

'The Sophies of this world?' Cassie asked.

He flashed her a look that was half-resentful and half-amused. 'You've never forgiven me for that, have you? You think I'm some kind of an ogre.'

She shook her head. 'I did, but if Sophie was what you said she was, I can hardly blame you for the way you treated her.'

He was silent for a moment. Then suddenly he said, 'It's easier that way. Safer.'

'Why?'

There was an even longer pause. A waiter was hovering, and Guy called him over and ordered another two brandies. When they had been brought he said, 'Because that way, you don't get hurt. And I've...No, it doesn't matter.' He drank half the brandy in one go. 'I don't know why I'm talking like this. Must be the drink making me careless.'

Cassie decided to jump in at the deep end; it was now or never, the only chance she might ever have to break through the barrier. 'You were going to say,' she prompted softly, 'that you've been hurt too much in the past to risk it again.'

The grey eyes flashed with a light that was alarmed and wary. 'Did someone tell you—' he began.

Cassie nodded. 'Anna. I know she shouldn't have betrayed a confidence, but—well, I was having a real go at you to her, and I was very angry, and she tried to explain.'

'And it all came out.' Guy smiled sadly. 'I don't mind. There's no reason why you shouldn't know, and it saves me the trouble of repeating the whole miserable story.' He took another, smaller sip of brandy. 'I'm over it all now, of course—have been for years—but a thing like that leaves its mark. And in this business I've met so many women who remind me of my ex-wife—greedy, grasping, easily dazzled by a bit of fame, with nothing in the way of a heart behind their pretty faces.' He laughed shortly. 'Sorry, I'm beginning to sound maudlin. I'm not, really; I've just learned to live with it, and to play them at their own game.'

'Because it's safer...'

'Because it's safer.' He stared down at his glass, and suddenly Cassie felt desperately sorry for him. He was a deeply unhappy man, and for the first time she fully understood the cynicism and bitterness that drove him to behave the way he did.

Abruptly he looked up. 'Finish your brandy, and let's get back to the house,' he said. 'We can have some coffee and see if there are any corny films on TV.'

'Busman's holiday,' said Cassie, and emptied her glass. Guy settled the bill, and they left the restaurant.

The fresh air outside struck them like a wave of cool water, and, still feeling a little light-headed, Cassie stumbled on the kerb of the pavement. Guy reached out and caught her, steadying her, and as his fingers closed on her arm she felt a sharp, almost electric thrill run through her. Suddenly she was thrown back to the disastrous evening in Guy's suite, when they had stood together by the window looking down on the lights of London, and she had felt that same strange tingling. She had been afraid of it then, but now...

They were back at the house within minutes, but the television did not go on. Instead Guy made coffee and they sat together on the sofa under the amber light of a single lamp. And when Guy's arm slid across the back of the sofa and around her shoulders, it seemed the most natural thing in the world to move closer to him, until her head was on his shoulder and she could feel the warmth of his body and catch the slight scent of his skin and hair in her nostrils.

His other hand reached across and touched her face, tracing a gentle line down the curve of her cheek. He said simply, 'Cassie.' And when she lifted her head instinctively, his mouth found hers with a quiet intensity that sent a shock of happiness through her entire being. They drew apart, and she saw his eyes, dark now as a stormy sea, gazing at her with a look they had never held before. All the coldness, the reserve, had gone from them; they almost seemed to plead with her. And then he was kissing her face, her neck, his hands clasping her against him until she thought he would crush her. Her arms slid around his neck and her lips sought his for a second time. The room seemed to fade into a soft, deep darkness around them, and everything was forgotten but the immediacy of that moment, so that they might have been the only two people in the world . . .

Guy's bedroom was suffused with the same amber light, the long curtains closed against the dark night outside. The wide bed seemed to welcome Cassie like a feathery cloud as she sank on to it, and when at last she and Guy lay together among the freshly-aired linen, she felt as though her heart could burst with sheer joy.

His hands caressed her, very gently, exploring every curve of her body as he whispered her name. He was as brown as she, his body lithe and warm, and his black hair made him look almost gipsyish in the half-light, strange and mysterious. His arm slid round her and he pulled her closely to him, firing her with his heat as he kissed her. She knew only that her whole being, right down to her soul, ached for him, and that she was lost in a happiness that she had never known in her life.

Guy's lips touched her ear. 'Oh, Cassie,' he whispered as his hair brushed her cheek, 'this is so different, so different. I've never known anyone like you, sweet Cassie . . .'

Cassie responded with all her heart. She could find no words to say, but the wave of feeling that poured from her was almost physical in its power. And in the moment when their bodies joined and became one she clung to Guy, welcoming his warmth and his weight that crushed her into the soft bed. The tears that had been welling up in her eyes overflowed and spilled down her cheeks. It was the only way she could express the joy she felt.

It was well past two in the morning, and the moon beyond the window was casting silvery patterns among the shadows of the dark room as Cassie lay watching Guy—her lover—as he slept. There was an almost childlike innocence about his face in repose and his black hair was tangled on the pillow as he breathed lightly.

Cassie knew there was no point in trying to sleep. Her mind was too full of thoughts, strange and new to her, flashing through her brain like bright beams of sunlight through a cloudy sky.

How long had she known, she asked herself? Had she suspected on the day she first met Guy that her true feelings were not what she had told herself they were, and that this man could awaken her to an intensity of emotion she had never known before? Certainly she had been frightened of those feelings for some time now, and tonight she had at last given way to the instinct that told her he was not what he appeared to be. Now she had seen the real man behind the mask, the human being under the cold guise, and she thought she understood.

She leaned across and touched Guy's cheek. He stirred, but did not wake, and she bent to kiss his brow lightly.

'Oh, Guy.' Her voice was a soft whisper; she was anxious not to disturb him, yet she had to say the words. 'I love you . . .'

10

Waking in the morning was a strange experience for Cassie.

She had hardly slept at all during the night—her mind was too full of the strangeness, the newness and the power of her new-found relationship with Guy— and she was fully awake by seven-thirty. Guy stirred an hour later, when the full brilliance of the sun was streaming in through the curtains, and for a fleeting moment as his grey eyes opened he seemed bewildered. Then he saw Cassie's face beside him on the pillow, and his mobile mouth relaxed into a smile.

'Hello,' he said. The word was cautious, exploratory and a little embarrassed. Cassie returned the smile.

'Hello yourself. Sleep well?'

'Better than I can ever remember.' Raising himself on one elbow he leaned across and kissed her. When they drew apart their eyes met, and after a minute Guy blinked and glanced down.

'I feel I ought to say something,' he said quietly. 'But I don't know what.'

Cassie laughed. 'Then say nothing. There's no need.'

He nodded gratefully, then, 'Would you like some breakfast?'

Cassie felt as though she could have eaten a banquet

single-handed at that moment and she accepted the offer eagerly.

'Okay. Wait here and you can have the luxury of tea in bed.' Guy slid out from under the blankets, and she watched him as he crossed the room and took a dressing-gown from the wardrobe. When he had gone she lay back, luxuriating in the warmth and comfort of not having to get up. She could hear him moving about downstairs and then, to her surprise, she heard him whistling. She'd never known him to do that before—usually when not actually talking or concentrating on something he was taciturnly silent. It was a good sign, a very good sign. With a sigh Cassie rolled over and smoothed her hand across the pillow where his head had been, smiling a secret smile. Somewhere in the back of her mind a small voice was asking, *What now? Where will you go from here?* But she ignored it. Now was not the time for such thoughts. *Let this moment last as long as possible*, she told herself, *and don't spoil it.*

Guy came back with a loaded tray, and they drank tea and munched toast, laughing when crumbs found their way into the bed. It seemed to Cassie that Guy's personality had undergone an extraordinary change overnight; he was relaxed, cheerful, and happy in an almost childlike way which brought back to her all her emotions of last night, building on them and making them firm. At last, at nine-thirty, he put the tray down and said reluctantly, 'Oh well, time to get up. We've got work to do.' A broad grin. 'That's what we came down here for, if you haven't forgotten!'

She pulled a face at him and climbed out of bed. She felt a little self-conscious as she gathered up her clothes, but Guy's gaze, following her as she moved about the room, was warm and admiring. He directed her to the shower, and she came out minutes later feeling refreshed and ready for anything. By ten, they left the house and started back for the village centre and the offices of Martin & Beresford.

The receptionist greeted them with a cheerful smile and said that Mr. Martin was expecting them and would they like to go straight up to his office? Guy knew the way and led Cassie up a flight of uncarpeted stairs with a high polish and through a heavy door into a neatly furnished office that seemed to be crammed from floor to ceiling with books and files.

Charles Martin rose to greet them. He was a little under forty, Cassie guessed, with fair hair that was starting to recede and modishly round spectacles. She was introduced, and Charles insisted that they join him for morning coffee. When it arrived, he leaned back in his swivel chair and said, 'Well, Guy, what's this all about?'

Guy told the story with help from Cassie, and when they had finished she pulled the two copied letters from her bag and laid them on the desk.

The solicitor read them through, then the fair brows behind the owlish glasses lifted. 'Good grief! You seem to have uncovered a rare old hornets' nest. I presume you now want legal advice on where to go from here?'

'Well, a little more than that, Charles,' Guy told him. 'We'd like you to handle it in an official capacity.'

Charles nodded slowly, still gazing at the letters. 'Is this the only concrete evidence you have?' he asked.

Cassie's heart sank; the question sounded ominous. 'So far, yes,' she replied, 'but there are other letters—a whole file full of them, in Van Hamer's office.'

'And no doubt more in Symes's,' Guy put in.

'I haven't had a chance to look at all of them,' Cassie went on, 'but I'm certain there'd be more than enough there to expose Hamer and Symes.'

'I'm sure there is. The only problem is how to get hold of them.' Charles smiled. 'I doubt if the gentlemen in question would be too keen simply to hand them over for the asking.'

'Are there any legal ways of getting them?' Guy wanted to know.

Charles gave him a sidelong look. 'We-ell, the only way would be to get a search warrant, and that presents two drawbacks. First, search warrants take time, even if we could be sure of having enough evidence to guarantee getting one. And I don't think time is really on our side. Second, it would mean involving the police, and I don't think they'd be particularly interested at this stage—there isn't enough clear evidence for them to step in. It's a bit of a vicious circle, I'm afraid; we can't get the letters—officially, that is—without police help, yet we can't enlist police help without the letters.'

'You said "officially",' Guy remarked.

Charles pursed his lips. 'Yes, I did, didn't I? That's all I can say, Guy. After all, a solicitor can hardly involve himself in anything underhand—it simply isn't ethical.' Suddenly his eyes twinkled. 'But that doesn't mean he can't turn a blind eye to any less—orthodox—*methods* his client may use to get his evidence, and be thankful for it.'

Guy grinned. 'Point taken. Okay, supposing we get the letters somehow. What then?'

'Ah, that's a very different matter. Then—and I mean immediately—we bring in the Fraud Squad, and I suspect that Messrs. Hamer and Symes will find themselves taking a long holiday.' He handed the letters back to Cassie, and added, 'I'll tell you what I'll do. I have no appointments for tomorrow that I can't cancel at short notice. You're going back to London today?'

'Yes.'

'Fine. Then you do what you can, and as soon as you have anything to go on, phone me. I'll come up post-haste, and with luck we can make a clean sweep.' The eyebrows lifted again. 'This is beginning to feel like a *Boys' Own* adventure—nothing as exciting has happened to me in a long time. It makes an enjoyable change from conveyancing and Trust administration!'

They laughed, and Charles rose to show them out. At the door, though, he said, 'Oh Guy—there was something else I wanted to talk to you about. That business about the common land at the back of your garden...'

Guy went back into the office, and Cassie, not wanting to get in the way, started slowly towards the stairs. She was idling in the passage when, through the half-open office door, she heard Charles's clear voice.

'You really pick 'em, don't you?'

Guy said something she couldn't catch, then the solicitor spoke again. 'That one's a right little raver, I'll bet! Cassie, didn't you say? How long do you think she'll last?'

Cassie's heart seemed to freeze. She was so stunned by what she had heard that again she did not catch Guy's reply—but then Charles laughed loudly.

In that moment it seemed that the ground shook

under her and opened up, pitching her into a black crevasse and shattering in an instant the beautiful dream that had been hers since the previous night. They were discussing her—that cruel remark of Charles's, then his ribald laughter at Guy's reply— what had Guy said to him?

A wall of red fury rose up in Cassie; she felt suddenly sick and could not bear to stay and hear any more. Running, she took the stairs at a perilous speed and leaned heavily against the wall at the bottom, biting her lip against the tears that threatened to spill down her cheeks.

Suddenly, her world was in ashes as her reason told her that everything between her and Guy had been a sham and a mockery. *What had he said to Charles that had made him laugh like that?* Something about her skill, or lack of it, in bed? Something to the effect that she was under his thumb and he had got her just where he wanted her...? Her imagination ran riot. But whatever the truth, one thing was clear. Guy Carver had been playing with her and he had won the game. He had used her, just as he used all the other girls in his life, and all the tenderness of the previous night, all the openness, was a cleverly-contrived way of winning her trust so that he could chalk up another conquest for his record.

God, MacRae, you're such a fool! she railed at herself. She should have listened to her earliest instincts and avoided him from the start. But he had been so clever...he had worked on her, slowly and surely, until he had convinced her that under the mask lay a real and warm human being. And she had fallen for it, hook, line and sinker!

Well, she had learned her lesson the hard way. She

had gone from dislike and mistrust to feelings of love for him—and real love, too, she reminded herself bitterly, not just an infatuation. And now, when she was on the pinnacle of happiness, he had thrown her down again. If this was his way of getting back at all women for what his wife had done to him, he must be very sick indeed, she thought.

Charles's door opened then and Guy came out. Hastily Cassie straightened and composed herself, working her face into an expression of disinterested calm. She would say nothing to Guy about what she had heard; she would simply preserve her dignity, or what was left of it in his eyes, and be polite but very cool with him. Let him work out for himself what was wrong—she was not going to tell him.

Guy smiled as he came down the stairs, and she returned it with a slight, emotionless quirk of her mouth.

'Well, that's settled!' he said. 'I must admit it's a relief to have the whole mess in official hands.'

'So we can go back to London,' Cassie said distantly.

He looked surprised. 'Are you in any hurry? I thought—'

'I'd like to get back, if you don't mind.'

'Well, okay—I suppose you're worried about Alan and work.'

She shrugged. 'The sooner we can get this sorted out the better it'll be for all of us.'

'True. But Cassie—'

She didn't wait to hear what he was going to say; she didn't want to hear it and she wasn't sure if she could maintain the calm pose in the face of any questions. Quickly she hurried towards the outer door of the office and was in the street before Guy caught up with her. He grabbed her arm, turning her to face him. 'Cassie, is something wrong?'

Taking a deep breath, she met his grey gaze. *Don't give way...*

'No, I'm fine,' she told him, her own eyes cold. 'I've just got a headache.' And thought, *liar!*

Guy looked at her doubtfully for another moment, then seemed to decide that there was no point pursuing the matter. 'All right,' he said resignedly. 'Back to London it is. Are you sure you feel up to travelling?'

'Perfectly.' She was thinking what a hypocrite he was, pretending such concern for her. If he knew that she had overheard Charles's remarks, she wondered, what would he do then? But no, she wouldn't tell him—not yet, anyway. Let him sweat for a while. And it would be safer from her own point of view to wait until she was calmer before there was any confrontation.

The silence between them was almost painful as the Aston-Martin nosed out of the village and started back towards London. Without waiting for Guy's approval, Cassie put a tape in the cassette player and turned the volume up to a level where conversation would have been impossible anyway. Then she sat back in her seat hugging herself and stared fixedly out of the window, trying to concentrate on the landscape and think about anything but the man beside her.

Guy drove fast, changing gear savagely on the bends as though he were trying to take out his frustration on the car. He was no longer cheerful; much of the old hardness had returned to the lines of his mouth and jaw. Cassie tried to tell herself that she was enjoying his discomfort, but deep down inside it gave her no satisfaction. It was just another symbol of her broken dream.

Thankfully there were no traffic hold-ups on the road, and in less than an hour and a half the car pulled up outside the Albury hotel.

Guy looked at Cassie. 'Do you want to get out here?'

'Yes, please,' She opened the door without waiting for him to say any more and almost ran into the hotel lobby. Once inside, she took the lift to her floor, went into her room and locked the door. Now she had things to do; she mustn't give way to the tears that still threatened her—she *mustn't* . . .

Quickly she picked up the phone, and a call to reception told her that Alan was filming a crowd scene in South London. Fine, she could get down to the set providing there was a car available, and hopefully get there before the lunch break ended so that she could do her explaining immediately. But before she went, there was one more call to make . . .

She dialled the hospital and enquired about Anna Loriot. Once again she had to go through the rigmarole of explaining who she was, and was told that Miss Loriot was much better and would be able to receive visitors probably on the following day. Thanking the receptionist and putting the phone down, Cassie rummaged through her wardrobe. She needed to change; her clothes reminded her too much of Guy and of what had happened.

She was pulling a fresh blouse out of the wardrobe when the self-control to which she had clung so desperately all morning gave way, and she sat down hard on her bed as tears poured down her cheeks.

If only she could truly believe that she hated him,

it would be so much easier. But that was a feeling that would have to be nursed and worked upon, and all the time it would be fighting against the memory of last night.

Suddenly angry, she wiped at her eyes and stood up, peering in the mirror of the vanity unit. Her mascara was smudged; quickly she cleaned it away as the last of the tears dried. Anger was her best weapon right now; it would keep her going when moments like this occurred. And she had to keep going. She must not give in.

With that thought in her mind she picked up the telephone again. 'Hello...I'd like to order a taxi as soon as possible, please...Yes, I'll be down in a couple of minutes. Thank you.'

And replacing the receiver, she turned back to the mirror to touch up her makeup.

Cassie arrived at the location scene just as the crew were going back to work after their lunch break. She saw Alan in conversation with two of the technicians and hurried towards him.

'Cassie!' His jaw dropped as he saw her. 'Where in God's name have you *been?*'

'Alan, I'm sorry,' Cassie said, 'I didn't have time to explain more fully, but it was very important. I've discovered something that—'

He didn't give her a chance to finish. 'Well, you're back now and that's what matters—I've been going spare without you! There's a million and one things that need doing.'

'Alan, *listen—*'

'So for starters could you go and help the continuity girl? We've got so many extras on the set today, the place is in chaos!'

'Alan—'

He paused for breath, then said, 'Look, Cass, save the explanation for later, okay? I think the weather's going to break, and we've got to get this scene completed before it does. You can tell me all about it this evening, all right?' And ruffling her hair he gave her a wink and hurried away.

Cassie sighed with exasperation. When Alan was in this sort of mood it was impossible to get through to him; he was completely absorbed in what he was doing, and nothing could get him out of it. The story would simply have to wait.

She made a face at Alan's departing back and went to find the continuity girl.

By evening, Cassie could have murdered Alan. He had not allowed her the chance to say a word to him all afternoon, and then when the crew returned to the hotel when work was finished, he promptly secreted himself in his suite with the assistant director and the chief lighting cameraman for a rapid conference. By the time this was over, it was time for the day's rushes to be shown, and so Cassie went along to the makeshift theatre feeling that she was about to boil over with frustration.

Luckily for her, she had been kept busy all day, and had had no time to brood on the events of the past twenty-four hours. Guy had not shown his face at the location site, as he was not needed, and when she returned to the hotel Cassie found to her relief that he was not around.

But as she walked into the room where the rushes were to be shown, the old feelings suddenly came back. If Guy should be there to see the day's shooting,

143

she knew she could not face him. As she bathed and changed in her room, the telephone had rung several times, but she had not answered it, afraid that it might be him.

She was a few minutes late for the rushes, and the room was dark when she entered. After a few moments her eyes grew used to the dimness, and she saw to her relief that Guy was not among the group of people who sat in front of the rigged-up screen.

Alan nodded to her as she came in, and when she sat down beside him he whispered, 'We're also going to see some of the last few days' shots, to make sure there aren't any continuity problems.'

Cassie's heart sank. That meant that whether she liked it or not she would be seeing Guy tonight, albeit only on the screen. But she just nodded and settled down to watch.

She soon realized that the clips being shown included a scene Guy had filmed with Janey Moore— a very poignant love scene. As soon as it started she felt uncomfortable, but she could not get up and walk out—it would look too obvious. So instead she sat and suffered in silence. Watching the image on the screen she felt her anger beginning to seep back. Guy's performance was superb—he was thoroughly convincing—and it brought back echoes of the previous night. The sweet things he had said to her as they made love—had he learned them all from scripts, perfected them so that to her unsuspecting mind they sounded genuine, meant for her alone? She felt disgusted, not only with him but also with herself for being such a fool and falling for the trick. Of course he could put on a brilliant performance, of course he had been able to con her into believing everything he put across—that was his profession, and for years he had been highly paid for it.

She lapsed into an unhappy reverie as the rushes progressed, and when the lights abruptly went up in the room and the screen flickered into blankness, she was startled. She raised her head to find Alan watching her curiously.

'Cass?' His voice was anxious. 'Are you all right?'

She realized that there were fresh tears on her lashes, and hastily she wiped them away. 'I'm fine,' she said.

'No you're not. Come on, tell me. You've been in a weird mood for days—what's eating you?'

Suddenly she couldn't face Alan with it all. She needed time, if only a few minutes, to compose herself, or what remained of her strength would crumble.

'I—I just have to go to my room, to get something,' she said lamely. 'I'll tell you when I come down. And Alan—there is something else. Something very important; I've been trying to talk to you about it for days, but—'

'I know, I've been too busy. All right, cookie— you go on upstairs, and I'll meet you afterwards in the Terrace Bar, okay?'

'Okay.' She gave him a weak, grateful smile and left the room.

On the ninth floor Cassie hurried along the corridor and unlocked the door of her room. She felt that she was on the edge of a real storm of crying, and if it was going to happen she wanted to go through it alone. It was, surely, only a natural reaction, and once it was out of the way and she had disguised her red eyes, she would feel a lot better.

She switched on the light and stepped into the room, then pushed the door to close it. But it would not close; something was jamming it. And in the moment before she turned, Cassie knew...

'Cassie.' Guy stood on the threshold, his hand holding the door against her efforts to shut it and his grey eyes burning with a light that was half angry and half uneasy. 'Cassie, I've got to talk to you—now.'

11

He came into the room, closing the door at his back, and leaned against it as though he thought she would make a dive past him and run out. Cassie stared at him, her cheeks burning as all her anger and bitterness welled up in her again, and then sharply she turned away.

'I don't think we've got anything to say to each other.'

'Nothing to say?' Guy repeated, astounded. 'When you suddenly turn cold on me without a single word of explanation? Cassie, what the hell's going *on?*'

Oh, you think you're so clever, Cassie thought. He was playing the injured and innocent party so well that for a moment she almost believed it. But only for a moment—and then her temper snapped.

'Don't play games with me, Guy Carver!' she retorted savagely. 'I'm not quite as stupid as you think!'

'Cassie—'

But now that her wrath had broken, she didn't even try to stem it. 'When you have private conversations about other people, you should learn to keep doors closed!'

'What on earth do you mean?' His eyes were wide; he took a step forward and Cassie backed off.

'You know perfectly well what I mean—or you would, if your memory wasn't so conveniently faulty!

I'm talking about this morning, in your solicitor friend's office, when you and he were having a good laugh about me behind my back!' And as he opened his mouth to protest she went on furiously, 'What did you tell him? That I could do with a few bedroom lessons? "A right little raver" he called me. Did you agree with him? Or did you tell him that it was just a one-night stand?' As she spoke her voice grew more bitter and she added challengingly, 'What did you say to him that made him laugh as if it was some dirty joke?'

Guy's face froze, then a look of astonishment spread over it.

'You've got it completely wrong—' he began.

'Wrong? Oh no—my ears are as good as anyone else's! You used me last night—you used me just like you've used all those other girls, and once you'd had your fun you thought you could get away with laughing about it behind my back! I should have known from the start. You just can't resist a challenge, can you? As soon as you knew I wasn't interested in you, you couldn't be happy until you'd proved how irresistible you are and got me into bed! God, I *hate* you!' She spat the last words with such venom that Guy took a step back. Steadying himself, he shook his head.

'Cassie, you've got it all so *wrong!* Just give me the chance to explain—'

'Oh, no! I'm not falling for that one! You conned me beautifully last night, Guy Carver, and I don't doubt you're very pleased with yourself. But if you think you can do it again, you can go to hell!'

'But—'

'I don't want to listen! Whatever you say, do you think I'd believe a word of it after what you've done!

148

Betraying me the way you did—I don't ever want to set eyes on you again!'

A terrible silence fell. Cassie had run out of words; there was no more she could say, it was all out. Aware that she was starting to shake all over she stared defiantly at him, daring him to make any further attempt to pacify her.

Guy didn't make the attempt. Instead he shrugged and looked away. 'All right,' he said, 'if you're not even willing to listen, then I won't bother to say anything. And if you don't want to see me again, that's all right by me—except for one thing.'

'What?' Cassie demanded, her voice dangerous.

Guy's eyes met hers, cold and serious. 'The little matter of a fraud.'

She had forgotten that in the upset of the moment, and he continued, 'Like it or not, we're both involved in this, and for the time being we need each other's help, though it goes against the grain to admit it. Have you spoken to Alan?'

'I'm just about to.' Even her voice was trembling now; it seemed bizarre to be talking so calmly in the wake of such a savage outburst.

'I'll come with you,' Guy said.

'No—'

'Yes, and don't argue. When this is all over and done with I'll have no more to do with you. But for Alan's sake we've got to stay on speaking terms for a while yet.'

Once again he had got to her biggest weakness— her loyalty to Alan. Giving him an angry glare she said, 'All right. I suppose I can't argue with that. I'm going to see him now.'

Guy stood back to let her go past, and together they

walked towards the lifts. They rode in chilly silence to the Terrace Bar. When the doors opened Guy said, 'You've got the letters?'

'I've got them.' And Cassie marched out of the lift without waiting for him and headed for the table where Alan was sitting.

Alan looked from Cassie to Guy and back to Cassie again. He was well aware of the almost physical tension between them and had guessed that it was connected with Cassie's earlier upset during the rushes, but at that moment he was too astounded by what they had just told him to pay attention to anything else.

He looked at the letters again—Cassie had shown them to him straight away to add weight to the story—and sat down hard.

'I think someone'd better get me a drink...' he said.

Cassie headed for the bar and, returning with a large scotch, was in time to hear Guy say, '...other letters in Hamer's office. Charles has said he can come up at short notice to put the legal proceedings in motion, but his hands are tied unless we can get hold of them.'

Cassie put the drink down, and Alan said, 'Thanks,' and gulped half of it. 'Well,' he added, gasping slightly as the liquor burned his throat, 'I—I'm at a loss for words. Good grief... Has Anna been told?'

'No,' Cassie replied, 'she was taken to hospital before I could say anything.'

Alan frowned. 'Better not to worry her about it yet, then.' He glanced at them both, and from the look in his eyes Cassie knew that he had already got over the first shock. Now, with the help of the scotch, he was thinking clearly and quickly. 'And anyway, the three of us—with your solicitor friend, Guy should be enough. Now, there's no legal way we can get those letters, right?'

'Right,' said Guy.

'Fine.' A broad grin spread over Alan's face. 'In that case, we'll just have to walk into that office and take 'em.'

With a half-smile Guy looked at Cassie, but she refused to meet his gaze.

'We can't bungle it, of course,' Alan continued. 'We'll only have the one chance, and if we get found out before we can get the letters Hammer'll sue us for theft and destroy the evidence at the same time. But I think there's a fairly foolproof way . . .'

Guy was following his line of thought. 'You mean you'll phone Hamer in the morning and ask him to meet you here, to make sure that he isn't in his office . . .'

'Right.' Alan's grin became even wider until he looked like a dog that had just succeeded in catching its first rabbit. 'And when he arrives he'll find us gone—to his place. Hey, I'm enjoying this! Playing Sexton Blake—oh come on, Cass,' seeing her face, 'it isn't that bad!'

She glared at him, knowing full well that he knew it wasn't the matter of Van Hamer that had upset her, and Alan had the good grace to redden slightly. He looked at Guy again. 'Well, it all happens tomorrow, then. I'll call Hamer first thing and persuade him to come down—don't worry, I'll cook up some believable excuse. And Guy, can you contact your friend and ask him to meet us here around lunchtime?'

'I'll do that,' Guy promised. Silence fell for a moment, then he seemed to realize that Cassie and Alan wanted to talk without a third party in earshot, and he stood up. 'I'll see you both in the morning.'

151

Alan said goodnight, and Cassie looked away. Guy left the bar, and as soon as he had gone Alan leaned across the table and took Cassie's hand.

'All right. Now are you going to tell Uncle Alan what it's all about?'

Cassie bit her lip. The last thing she wanted was to start crying in public. She shook her head. 'There's no point, Alan. There's nothing you can do anyway, so why drag it all up?'

'I can't answer that until I know what "it" is, can I?'

She managed a weak smile. 'I know. But I don't want to talk about it right now. I need a bit of time to think, that's all. But please don't worry that it's going to affect my work. I won't let it.'

Alan snorted. 'Hell, woman, do you think I care a damn about that? You're what matters, and you remember it!' He tugged gently on a hanging lock of her blonde hair. 'Now why don't you have a stiff drink and get an early night? Tomorrow's going to be a busy day. When it's out of the way, then maybe you'll feel more like a heart-to-heart.'

He was right, and she was grateful for the advice. 'Thanks, Alan. I'll do that.'

'And think of the adventure ahead, right?'

'Right.' It was the last thing she was thinking of, but there was no need to worry Alan by saying so. Better to let him think he had cheered her up. She rose. 'Goodnight, then. I'll see you in the morning.'

'Night night. Sweet dreams.' He winked at her as she left the table.

Cassie had one of the worst night's sleep of her life. All through the dark hours she was plagued by restless, half-waking dreams, and all the dreams concerned

Guy. One in particular recurred time after time, in which she was back at the house in Sussex, in the warm, softly-lit bedroom, with Guy's arms about her and his naked body pressed close to hers as he kissed her. After those dreams she woke to find the blankets in a tangle around her and once, when still half-asleep she reached out expecting to touch Guy's hair on the pillow beside her, she found only cold linen.

By six o'clock she knew she could not get back to sleep again, and she didn't want to. Though being awake meant facing reality, that was better than the disappointment of coming up from a beautiful dream to find nothing there. So she switched on the light, turned on the radio for the early morning news and sat in bed for a while, grimly determined not to think about unhappy subjects.

There was little to do for the first few hours of that morning. Alan had contrived—with some help from the weather, which was sending down a torrent of rain by eight-thirty—that there should be no filming that morning; but waiting for ten o'clock, when Van Hamer would be in his office, was frustrating. At last, though, the hour arrived, and by ten-fifteen the producer had been persuaded to meet Alan at the hotel for an important and urgent discussion about the film.

Alan was jubilant as he put the phone down. 'He'll be here in an hour,' he told Cassie. 'So if we arrange to get there five minutes before he's due here, everything should go as smoothly as clockwork.'

'And what happens when he finds out you're not here?'

'Well, it'll be a bit late then, won't it? Providing Guy's solicitor arrives when he says he will, our Mr. Hamer's going to have a lot of explaining to do before today's out.'

Cassie nodded. She wasn't too keen on the idea of marching into the film company offices and demanding the files, but knew that there was no other way to get them.

'Have you seen Guy this morning?' Alan asked. 'We need him too—I've got to find out when that Martin bloke's turning up.'

'I haven't seen him.' Cassie's voice was sharp, giving her away, and Alan gave her an odd look.

'Sorry. Was that tactless?'

'I can't very well deny his existence, can I?' Cassie muttered. There was no point in pretending that Guy wasn't the cause of her unhappiness; but she only hoped that Alan wouldn't choose this moment to start probing again.

To her relief, he didn't. Instead he asked the hotel receptionist to page Guy, and minutes later the three of them met in the lobby.

Guy gave Cassie a cautious greeting, which she returned with a frozen ghost of a smile, and Alan explained what had happened. Guy, as it turned out, had phoned Charles on the previous evening, and the solicitor would be arriving at the Albury at about twelve noon, traffic permitting.

'Well, that's about it.' Alan rubbed his hands together. 'It only remains for us to do the dirty deed...'

And so a little after eleven Guy's car pulled up outside Hamer's Soho office. It had occurred to Cassie that perhaps the other directors might not be too keen on a group of strangers rummaging through their files, but Alan, when she put her objection to him, dismissed it, telling her that this was only a subsidiary office where Hamer himself and his small staff worked. His co-directors were housed at another address.

'Come on,' he urged her, 'don't go getting cold feet at this stage!'

'I'm not!' she retorted indignantly. 'Just trying to be practical, that's all. Who was it who said we mustn't make a mess of this chance?'

'Touché.' Alan grinned. 'Right, henchmen, let's go in and do our worst!'

Luckily the receptionist on the desk didn't know Alan by sight; she was the more helpful of the two girls Cassie had seen before, and when Alan asked if they could fetch a file from the office on Mr Hamer's behalf, she gave them a sunny smile and told them to go straight on up.

As soon as she saw the secretary sitting in the office, Cassie felt that her guilt must be written all over her face. But the girl obviously saw nothing untoward, for as soon as Alan explained their 'mission', she was only too eager to be helpful. Cynically, Cassie noted the way she looked at Guy with an almost awestruck expression, and knew that they'd have no trouble from her; she had other things on her mind.

Go on, seduce her, why don't you? she thought savagely. *Play the great lover and let Alan and me get on with our side of it . . .* Suddenly she realized that Guy was watching her, and quickly she composed her face, which had been becoming angry and miserable. Behind her, Alan hovered.

'Cass, you know more about these things than I do—which file was it Mr. Hamer said we needed?'

He spoke for the secretary's benefit, and Cassie started. 'Oh—sorry, I was daydreaming. This drawer here, I think,' she said, opening it. 'Yes—that's the file.'

She pulled it out and Alan took it gingerly, as though expecting it to be red-hot. For a few seconds he stared at it, hardly able to believe that they had succeeded so easily. Then he pulled himself together and gave the secretary his sweetest little-boy smile. When Alan smiled like that, no one could believe him capable of telling the smallest fib.

'Thank you very much,' he said. 'Sorry to have disturbed you, but now we've got this it means we can get on with the important stuff.'

How right you are, Cassie thought, trying to keep back the urge to smile at Alan's outrageous nerve.

'And please thank Mr. Hamer for me,' he added, his eyes twinkling. 'I'm very grateful to him.'

That was sailing a bit close to the wind, and Cassie prodded Alan in the ribs. 'We should get back to the set,' she said pointedly.

'Of course.' Alan was enjoying himself at this game, but nonetheless let her lead him out of the office. As they walked down the stairs, Cassie was dreading meeting Hamer returning, but they gained the car without any trouble.

Guy slid into the driver's seat and started the engine. 'You did that magnificently, Alan,' he said. 'I needn't have bothered to come.'

'You're our getaway driver, remember?' Alan reminded him. 'Anyway, three's a lucky number, right, Cass?' He looked over his shoulder to where she sat in the back, and she nodded.

'Right. But do we have to hang around now we've got the wretched letters?'

'We certainly don't. Alan settled the file on his knee. 'Okay, let's get back. And then we can celebrate!'

12

'It's perfect!' Charles Martin slapped his hand down on the bulging file in front of him and looked from Guy to Alan. 'Everything we could possibly need to prove a massive fraud.' He adjusted his glasses with a smile and added, 'The police are going to love this—it'll make their job very easy indeed.'

The solicitor had arrived half an hour previously, and had wasted no time at all. A brief glance through the file had been enough to confirm everyone's suspicions, and he had immediately telephoned Scotland Yard. The Fraud Squad had been slightly dubious at first, but, on learning that Charles was a solicitor and that he had all the necessary concrete evidence literally to hand, they had promised to send an investigating officer without delay.

Cassie stood a little apart from the three men in Alan's suite, hovering near the window on the pretext of watching for the police, but in reality anxious to keep out of the way. She had dreaded the prospect of coming face to face with Charles again, uncertain that she could stop herself from either losing her temper or bursting into tears on sight of him, but her attempts to wriggle out of this conference had been firmly blocked by Alan. She was, he told her in a no-nonsense tone, their star witness, and if she thought she would be allowed to miss out on all the fun, she had another think coming. It had been on the tip of Cassie's tongue to tell him the real reason for her reluctance, but there seemed little point. Alan was no fool—he was well aware that something was very wrong between her and Guy, and even though he had no idea of Charles's connection, she doubted if any pleas would carry weight. And besides, even if they did, the whole story would take far too long to explain. Time was not on her side.

And so she had managed, by what she felt must be some miracle, to keep a calm face in front of Charles. He obviously had no idea of what had happened—he and Guy had not had a chance to talk privately together since his arrival—and so long as it stayed that way, Cassie felt she could cope. But every time the solicitor spoke to her, or smiled at her in his assured, professional way, she wanted nothing more than to clench her fist and hit him.

She realized then that Alan was speaking, and turned her attention from the window to listen.

'My one worry,' he said, leaning forward and riffling the papers in the file as if he couldn't quite believe they were real, 'is that Hamer might get wind of what's going on, and bolt for it before the police make any move.'

Charles smiled indulgently. 'I think you've been reading too many crime novels, Mr. Blythe! Villains like Hamer don't usually go in for melodramatics. I mean, he's hardly likely to go back to his office, have a showdown with his secretary over the missing file, and make his escape in a convenient helicopter, is he?'

Alan looked annoyed, but Guy came to his rescue. 'I think Alan's got a point, Charles. Apparently Hamer was none too pleased when he got here this morning and found Alan missing. It might have aroused his suspicions—and if it has, chances are that he'll think to check that file. Once he knows it's gone, and who took it, he's not going to hang around.'

'No,' Alan put in, 'and of course he'll warn Andrew Symes. Which means that Symes will destroy all his copies of the letters.'

Charles made a dismissive gesture. 'That's neither here nor there. What we've got is more than enough to implicate the pair of them. If we—'

He was interrupted by Cassie, who had returned to the window and was staring down into the West End traffic. A large, maroon Rover had just drawn up by the hotel entrance, and she said, 'I think they've arrived.'

Guy immediately stood up and came to the window to look out. If he noticed the way Cassie quickly drew back as he approached, he said nothing, only stared out and down.

'Yes, it's them,' he said.

'Right!' Charles gathered up the papers and headed for the door, with Guy on his heels. They disappeared into the corridor, but Cassie hung back. Suddenly she felt very tired, and only wanted the chance to be alone for a while. She didn't care about being in at the kill, or about the praise that would be coming her way for her part in the affair. She only wanted to be away from Guy, away from Charles Martin, away from everyone.

Slowly she started across the room, wondering if she could slip back to her own room without anyone seeing her. Then a voice behind her said, 'Cass?'

She'd forgotten Alan, who had not left with the other. He was watching her, arms akimbo, and his eyes were full of sympathy.

'Come on, girlie,' he said quietly. 'What's eating you?'

She looked away, unreasonably angry with him because his kind tone had been just the trigger she had been dreading. One gentle word was enough to start the tears prickling at the back of her eyes. 'Nothing,' she said, trying to force her voice not to quaver. 'I'd just...rather go to my room and leave all of this to you.'

'Like hell you will!' Alan protested, and then, in a vigorous tone that she knew was meant to buck her flagging spirits, he added, 'You're the heroine of the day, Cass, and I for one am *not* going to let you miss out on the fun!'

'Fun?' she said, staring bitterly at him.

Alan looked discomfited. 'Well...okay, love, I know you're not in the mood for fun, but—it'll get your mind off whatever it is that's chewing you up right now, won't it? Old Boss-Man isn't going to let his favourite girl hide herself away and brood. Come on, you're coming downstairs with me—and that's an order!'

There was no point trying to explain to Alan. In his well-intentioned way he was doing what he thought best for her welfare, and she had to be grateful to him. And in a sense he was right—brooding would get her nowhere. In a sudden burst of determination Cassie decided that she would show Guy Carver that she didn't care, that he hadn't hurt her. Or at least, she would try.

With a smile she said, 'Okay, I give in,' and followed Alan out of the room.

Cassie had never met an English police inspector before, and subconsciously she had been expecting a sort of cross between Sherlock Holmes and the bluff, shrewd but ruthless men in trilbys and raincoats portrayed on film. The Scotland Yard detective who met her and Alan in the Terrace Bar was a complete contrast to all her ideas. Small, lightly built and urbane, he looked more like a City businessman than a dedicated crime-solver. By the time the pair arrived in the bar, Charles Martin had already handed over the file, and the Inspector was poring over it, his expression unreadable. They waited in silence, during which Cassie looked everywhere but in Guy's direction, until after a few minutes the Inspector looked up and said, 'Right.'

Alan's face became eager. 'Are you going to arrest them, Inspector?' he asked.

The Inspector gave him a long-suffering glance, which he quickly overlaid with a pleasant smile. 'I'd just like to check a few facts, sir, to make sure I've got the record straight. We could do ourselves more harm than good by jumping the gun.'

Alan started to protest at what seemed, to him, an unnecessary delay, but Charles waved him into silence. He shifted impatiently from one foot to the other while the detective asked Cassie to repeat every snippet of conversation she had overheard, and questioned her closely as to precisely when and how her suspicions had been aroused. He then made her relate the story of her visits to Van Hamer's office, and when she came to the part about that morning's sortie to steal the file, he raised an amused eyebrow.

'That wasn't exactly very law-abiding of you, was it, Miss MacRae?'

Alan opened his mouth to jump to Cassie's rescue, but Guy beat him to it. 'She had no choice, Inspector, as far as I can see—none of us did. As Charles pointed out, without that file we didn't have enough evidence to interest your department, and Hamer was hardly likely to hand it over to us for the asking. Personally, I'm certain that if it hadn't been for Cassie we'd never have stood a hope in hell of exposing these two.' He glanced at Cassie then, perhaps wondering if his words had had a constructive effect on her, but was met with a coldly furious stare. At that moment he was the last person on earth she wanted as her champion, and she was angry that he had not kept quiet and allowed Alan to defend her.

The Inspector looked from one to the other. 'Obviously, sir, that's quite true, although it's the kind of point defence counsels are inclined to make a meal of. But in this case, I don't think it'll be a legitimate objection, when the weight of this evidence is taken into account.' He closed the file, and tucked it under his arm. 'I think that's all I need from you for the time being.'

Alan was as excited as a schoolboy. 'Then you're going to arrest them?'

The Inspector smiled. 'Yes. Though I'm afraid it won't be as dramatic as these scenes usually are in your profession.' He turned to speak to them all generally. 'I'd be grateful if you would all stay in the hotel until I come back. There'll be a fair number of loose ends to tie up—statements and suchlike. And I'll make sure this is kept in a safe place.' He brandished the file, then with a nod to the company, left the bar.

Alan stared after him, and Cassie knew what he was thinking even before he spoke.

'I'd love to see Hamer's face when they pick him up...'

Guy nodded agreement, and the two glanced at each other as the same thought occurred to them both.

'We could use my car,' Guy said.

'Yes... and we wouldn't get in the way. Nothing illegal about it, is there, Charles?'

The solicitor grinned. 'It's a free country. No law can stop you driving into the West End.'

'Right!' Alan rubbed his hands together delightedly. 'Then let's get moving, or it'll be all over before we get there. Charles, are you coming with us?'

Charles shook his head. 'No, no—professional etiquette; it would look too partisan. You can tell me all about it when you get back.'

'Cassie?' Alan asked. 'Coming to see the show?'

'No.' Cassie stated flatly.

Guy looked disappointed. 'Why not? It'll be—'

'No.' She interrupted him, and her tongue was so savage that both Guy and Alan thought better of pressing her any further. They hurried away in the direction of the hotel garage, and as they went Charles chuckled and said to Cassie,

'They're just like a couple of school kids, aren't they?'

Cassie didn't answer him. Now that the furore seemed to be all over, she had lapsed back into a sense of futile misery—and the presence of Charles Martin was only adding to her anger and unhappiness. Suddenly she didn't care about being polite. One more minute in Charles's company, and she knew she would say something she might regret.

She turned on her heel and walked out of the bar, leaving Charles staring after her in complete bewilderment. And as she crossed the lobby she heard the sound of tyres squealing as Guy's Aston-Martin hurtled out into the busy road on its way to Soho.

Guy and Alan were back in less than an hour, jubilant, and Alan came straight to Cassie's room, where she had been since they left. He burst in without knocking to find her lying on the bed. For a moment he was worried, but when she looked up and he saw that she was dry-eyed, he relaxed. All the same, he didn't like the cold, almost haunted look in her eyes.

He sat down on the bed, his face flushed. 'My god, girl, you don't know what you missed!' he crowed.

For his sake Cassie tried to summon up a show of interest. 'Gon on,' she said, 'tell me all!'

Alan launched off into his story. Apparently they had arrived at Hamer's office only half a minute behind the police car—due, apparently, to some reckless driving on Guy's part—and had stopped a few yards away, so that they could watch without being obtrusive themselves. By some extraordinary chance, as the Inspector climbed out of his car, Van Hamer had emerged from the office building, and so the ensuing scene had taken place in the street.

Guy and Alan had not been able to hear any of the conversation, but it was obvious that the Inspector had wasted no time with any preamble, for within seconds the colour had drained from Van Hamer's face and he had started to gesture in a blustering way.

'It was incredible,' Alan said animatedly. 'The Inspector guy must have been doing it all by the book, reading the caution or whatever they do here, because he stood there looking officious and made some kind of a speech. And you know what? Hamer tried to run for it!'

Despite herself, Cassie was fired by his enthusiasm. 'You're kidding!' she said.

'No, really! It was just like something out of Hollywood! Anyway, it didn't get him anywhere—there was a bit of a scuffle, then they bundled him into the car and whisked him away. Christ, you should have seen his face!'

'What happened then?' Cassie asked.

'Well, we drove round to Symes's place to see what was happening there, but they must have radioed another police car to pick him up, because by the time we got there he'd been carted off. Oh, by the way— there's a horde of coppers downstairs in the lobby— arrived the same time as we did, and they want to talk to us all. They're going to turn Hamer's suite over— the hotel manager's tearing his hair out!'

'I'm not surprised.' Cassie could imagine the poor man's reaction to this sudden invasion of his hotel by the forces of law. But the prospect of having to answer another set of questions daunted her—she felt tired and depressed, and not at all in the mood for keeping up any pretences. 'Do I have to see the police now?' she asked plaintively.

'Can't be helped, love.' Alan looked more closely at her, studying the tight lines around her eyes and mouth. 'Come on—put some warpaint on and let's get it over with.' He stood up as she too reluctantly rose and reached for her makeup bag, then added very firmly, 'And when this is all finished, I want a few private words with you.'

She gave him a weak smile. It would be a blessed relief to be able to talk to Alan at last, and to unburden herself a little. He would understand, and he would do anything he could to help her.

'Tell them I'll be down in a minute,' she said.

By the time Cassie stepped out of the lift into the hotel lobby, the general chaos had been increased by another and totally unexpected event.

She did not see the ambulance draw up at the hotel entrance, but when the doors burst open and a familiar voice cried out,

'*Alors!* What is this—are we at war?' she spun round in delighted astonishment.

'*Anna!*'

The little Frenchwoman stood in a dramatic pose in the doorway, flanked by two young ambulancemen both of whom seemed to be half-dazed. She was wrapped from neck to ankles in an enormous fur coat which virtually swamped her, and only her exquisitely made-up face and bright dark eyes were visible in the frame of the vast mink collar.

Cassie ran towards her. 'Anna, how lovely to see you!'

The little woman reached out a black-gloved hand and took Cassie's fingers in a strong, warm grip. '*Chérie!* So at least there is *someone* here to welcome me!'

'Oh Anna! We didn't expect you to be let out so soon. Are you all right? How do you feel? Cassie's questions came out in a great rush of breath.

'Ahh, these doctors! They do not know anything about anything! They starve me and they maltreat me—*tiens,* they will not even allow my hairdresser to come, so that I must sit in bed looking like the haystack! Today I tell them; I have had enough, and if they do not let me out of their Bastille at once, I shall make hell of their lives! So, they let me go, and I am back!' As she spoke she treated the two ambulance attendants to a queenly glare, but her eyes were twinkling. 'But *chérie*—what is happening here? What fun have I missed, and what are all those men?'

'Police,' Cassie hissed in her ear.

Anna's voice rose almost to a squeak and she repeated loudly, *'Police?* Then you—*alors*, you have—what is the phrase—you have blow the whistle on the villainous Hamer!'

Trying not to laugh, Cassie said, 'Yes, we've blown the whistle. They've both been arrested, and now the Fraud Squad are looking over Van Hamer's suite. I've got to go and give them a statement.'

'A statement? Then I too shall give them a statement, and such a statement! When I tell them what I think of that odious worm, their ears shall be ringing for a week! Where is the man in charge?' And brushing aside the anxious attendants she swept a little unsteadily across the lobby.

Cassie gave the two ambulancemen a sympathetic smile. 'I wouldn't bother arguing with her,' she said. 'It's not worth it!'

13

Anna looked fondly at Cassie from the armchair in which she sat, and said, 'So, *chérie*, you are the heroine, yes?'

Cassie returned her look with a warm smile. Now that the furore was over, she felt drained and exhausted. She had spent most of the afternoon going over her statement with the Inspector, until at last, to her relief, he was satisfied that all the facts tallied. For the rest of the day, the hotel had been swarming with police who wanted to question everyone who could possibly have anything to add. And of course Anna had been in the thick of it, ignoring her doctor's strict instructions that she should not exert herself in any way. Cassie had felt quite sorry for the police inspector by the time she had finished with him—to hear her lecturing him on his duty and her opinions, anyone would have thought that he, and not Van Hamer, was the culprit in this crime.

Alan, too, had been in on everything. From what he could gather—as he had told Cassie—the police had found no further evidence in Hamer's suite, but the papers they already had were more than enough to secure a conviction. Among the documents which Cassie had not previously seen were two sets of contracts made out to Alan, Anna and Guy, and these had supplied the vital missing link. Hamer had certainly set his plan up very cleverly. He had planned to cheat the three out of a large proportion of the money which the film company had agreed to pay them, and had drawn up—with Symes's help—contracts in which they had agreed to take a far lower sum than was actually due to them. His co-directors, as far as the police could tell, had no idea of what he was doing; they had signed the original contracts, and then Hamer had forged their signatures on his own revised version of the documents, which he had presented to the three people involved. They had signed in good faith. And Hamer had engineered it so that he would be responsible for actually making the payments to the cast and director, and so, had it not been for Cassie, the balance would have gone neatly into his pocket, with a large backhander for Symes and no questions asked.

Now, it only remained to clear up the mess that their attempted crime had caused—although that was to be no small task. Even now Cassie could hardly believe that it had all happened. Sitting with Anna in her suite, she felt as though she was slowly emerging from a bad dream. It was hard to accept that the nightmare was a reality.

'I'm not a heroine, Anna,' she said with a half-smile. 'I'm certain someone would have uncovered it anyway. All I did was set the wheels in motion.'

Anna made a dismissive gesture. 'Nonsense! You are either too modest, or a great fool if you think that! We should all bless you—thanks to you, we are all to be much wealthier than we thought!' Her eyes twinkled. 'Alan must raise your salary—double it—and I shall tell him so!'

At that moment there was a knock on the door, and Alan put his head round.

'Speak of the devil!' said Anna. 'Come in, Alan, come in.'

'Speak of the devil? Who's the devil?' Alan asked.

'You are.' Anna motioned him towards a chair. 'I was just telling Cassie that you will double her salary, or I shall want to know the reason why not!'

Alan laughed. 'She'll get that all right. But, Cassie—I want to talk to you. It's important.'

Behind the smile his eyes were worried, and Cassie stood up. 'Anna, if you'll excuse me...'

'Certainly, *chérie*. But you will come back?'

'Of course.' She followed Alan out of the suite, and he headed for the lifts. 'Come down to the bar with me, Cass. I need a drink.'

They reached the Terrace Bar, and when they were seated at a table with a double whisky apiece (Cassie had tried to refuse, but he insisted), Alan looked at her and said,

'Cass, I know this is going to come like a bolt out of the blue, but—we're going back to Australia.'

'Going back?' she echoed, astounded. 'But Alan—'

'I know, I know; what about the film? Well, it's like this—it's going to take one hell of a long time before this financial chaos can be sorted out, and I've just been told that all work on the film's to be halted at least until it's cleared up. To be frank, no one knows yet whether it'll even be completed. Personally I think it will; they've sunk enough money into it already to make it crazy to give up. But before we can roll again, there were going to be endless weeks of talks and wrangles. And I'm not too keen on the idea of sitting around twiddling my thumbs in London while the money boys waffle. So I'm taking you back home, where we can at least do some honest work.'

It made sense. But something inside Cassie seemed to shrivel as he spoke. To go home—yes, it would be lovely; she was homesick, and the thought of seeing her family and friends again was wonderful. But if she left now, so much would be unresolved. She would leave so much pain behind her.

She stared down into her glass. 'Yes, Alan. It's the best thing to do.'

'But you're not happy about it, are you?'

She thought about that for a few moments. In so many ways she *did* want to get as far away from Guy as possible; it would help the bitterness to heal. But underlying her anger was a terrible emotional pain. She had fallen in love with Guy and despite everything that had happened she found it impossible to fall out of love with him as quickly. Part of her still believed that there must be an explanation for his behaviour; that he was not as callous as her own ears and eyes had told her. But she fought that feeling, knowing that it could only lead to more trouble. And whatever happened, she couldn't bear to let him hurt her again. All right, so she would go back to Australia and try to get over him; she would succeed, in time. But what would happen if and when work on the film was resumed? They would return to London and she would have to face Guy and all that he meant to her over again.

Yet that surely was better than spending the next few weeks here. At home, she would at least have the chance to heal her bruised emotions...

'Yes,' she said to Alan, who was still waiting for an answer to his question. 'I am happy about it. In fact...I want to go home.'

171

Alan didn't reply at first. He had watched the play of emotions across her face, and knew that she was probably closer to breaking point than she had ever been. He knew, too, that he wasn't the most subtle of men and that it would be all too easy to say the wrong thing, but he was very fond of Cassie, and his conscience was pricked by the fact that he had not had the time to get to the bottom of what was troubling her. It didn't take a genius to guess the basics, but the details—and in particular the events of the last twenty-four hours—were still a mystery to him.

There was only one thing to do, he decided. No point in hedge-hopping around the subject; that would be out of character, and would put her on edge. He must do what he usually did—jump in at the deep end and hope that the water wasn't too cold.

So he said firmly, 'Nuts.'

Cassie looked up, startled. 'Wh—what do you mean, Alan?'

'Just what I said. Nuts. You *don't* want to go home—or at least, if you do, it's just because at home you can hide from everything. But hiding doesn't do you any good, Cass. In the long run, it only makes things worse.'

He didn't know how she would react to that, but when she *did* react he was dismayed, for she abruptly burst into tears.

'Hey, Cassie!' Alan didn't know quite what to do; in all the time she had worked for him he had never seen her in anything approaching this state. Cassie wasn't a cryer—or at least, she never had been until now.

'I'm sorry...' she sniffed, trying to dry her eyes, but the tears kept on flowing. It was the first time that Cassie had really been able to let herself go, discounting the awful hours when she had been alone. Awkwardly Alan gripped her shoulder and shook it gently. 'Come on—this isn't like my Sydney girl! You're going to tell me exactly what's wrong, and I'm going to put it right for you!'

Through her tears Cassie couldn't help laughing, though it wasn't much of a laugh. Then her smile faded and she said, 'You can't put it right, Alan. No one can.'

'Now you're being melodramatic. It's Guy Carver, isn't it?'

A pause, then she nodded.

'You've gone and done it, haven't you? Fallen for him?'

Another nod, then Cassie said sadly, 'The trouble is, Alan, it's not just an infatuation. I've had those before—everyone does—and I can cope with that sort of thing. But this—'

Alan didn't argue with her. Even if he had believed it was an infatuation he couldn't have convinced her of it, and anyway, he was shrewd enough to have seen the signs of something more genuine. He felt deeply sorry for Cassie—and angry with the man who had upset her.

'What's he done?' he asked.

It was bluntly put, but it had the effect of shaking Cassie out of her misery enough to think more clearly. She wasn't embarrassed about telling Alan the details; her only fear was that she might bore him with them. But Alan was insistent, and so by degrees the whole story came out—of how Cassie had been determined to dislike the young actor, of how, despite herself, her opinion had changed gradually as she got to know him better. And finally there was the account of the journey to Sussex, and of the brief explosion of happiness that had turned to disaster when she overheard the conversation in Charles Martin's office.

Alan's face clouded as she related this, until by the time she finished his expression was thunderous. 'The dirty little—'he began, then stopped himself as he realized he was in mixed company. 'I could go right now and throttle the pair of them with my bare hands!'

Cassie, however, was having an attack of cynical realism, and she said, 'That's stupid. If you want to be brutal about it, they're not to blame. It's my fault, for letting myself be gulled so easily.'

'Hell, you can't take that attitude!' Alan exploded. 'I mean, I know I'm no saint, but I'd never treat *any* woman like that, let alone a woman like you! Guy Carver's not so dumb that he couldn't have known you were keen on him! And to walk all over you, wipe his feet on you and then brag about it to his slimy friend—that's diabolical!' Seething, he stood up and paced round the table, his hands thrust deep into his pockets.

Aware that people in the bar were staring at them, Cassie waved him hastily back to his seat. When he had subsided, she said, 'Well, there's nothing I can do about it, is there?'

Alan couldn't dispute that. He sighed. 'I don't know, Cass. I honestly don't know.'

'So the best thing of all would be to go home to Australia.'

Alan shook his head despairingly. 'I don't know about that, either. I mean, what good will it do? You won't forget him that quickly—not if I know you. And then we'll probably have to come back to England in a month or two, and it'll start up all over again.' What's the good of running away?' He looked at her, his eyes full of sympathy.

'Maybe you're right,' she replied slowly. 'But at least in Sydney I'll have a *chance* to forget. There'll be work to do, and all my friends to see, and ... well, it's *home*, it's familiar. It's the only way, Alan. There's no better alternative.'

She was right, he knew, but still his nature rebelled against her resignation. 'God, if I could get my hands on him—' he started.

'No, Alan, don't say that. It won't do either of us any good, and it'll probably start me off defending him, or something dumb like that. I want to go home. It's for the best.'

Alan calmed himself with an effort. He would have given a lot to be able to champion Cassie right now, to play the big brother that he had always been to her. But she was right. It was for the best.

'All right, Cass,' he said gently, 'we'll both go home.' And when she didn't answer he reached out and took her chin in his hand, tilting her face up. 'Don't worry, love. It'll be all right.' And he leaned forward and kissed her on the forehead.

Alan managed to get seats on a flight to Sydney leaving the following day, and Cassie took that news with a mixture of relief and anguish. Sitting in her room later that evening she had to fight back an impulse to seek out Guy and tell him to his face that they were leaving, but knew it would be a foolish thing to do. If she confronted him she might be all too vulnerable. Best just to leave without a word and to avoid him until it was time to get into the car for the airport. And once she was on the plane, the whole matter would be out of her hands.

She looked around the room. Better start packing, or she would end up having to do it all in five minutes tomorrow. Or perhaps that would be just as well, for if she was in a last-minute hurry she would have no time to think.

She decided to compromise. Pack the things she was most likely to forget now, and leave the major things, such as clothes, till tomorrow.

When someone knocked on the door of her room, she called out 'Come in,' expecting it to be Alan. But when a less familiar voice said, 'Miss MacRae...?' she straightened and turned round in surprise.

Her visitor was Charles Martin. He stood on the threshold looking uneasy, and, seeing him, Cassie frowned. 'Mr. Martin. Did you want something?' She could barely bring herself to be civil to the man after what had happened and her eyes were hard as she looked at him.

Charles came into the room, closing the door. 'I thought I'd better come up, as I heard you were leaving tomorrow.'

'That's right.'

'Well...it's—er—about the court case. When it comes up, you'll be needed as a prime witness—you and Mr. Blythe, that is.'

'I see. That shouldn't present any problems. By the time it comes to court, Alan and I will probably be back in England anyway.'

'Oh. Fine.' Charles hesitated, and she knew before he spoke that that was not the real reason for his visit.

Suddenly he took a deep breath and said, 'Actually, Miss MacRae, I really came to apologize to you.'

She stopped what she was doing. 'Apologize?'

'Yes—for what happened the other day in my office...the things I said.'

A frosty smile curved Cassie's mouth. 'I think if

anyone ought to apologize for that it's Guy, not you.'

'That's just the point,' Charles said unhappily. 'I've been talking to Guy. He told me that you think he was saying things about you behind your back. The truth is, he wasn't. It was all my fault, I—well, you know what men are; they love to talk, and sometimes the talk gets a bit personal . . . I'm not proud of what I said, but I can't deny that I said it, because I was curious. I know what Guy's usually like with women, so I thought . . . well, I thought he'd take it all in good part, because I assumed you were just another . . . well, I was wrong. When I said what I did, Guy tore me off a strip for it, and I—I laughed. I didn't take him seriously. But now that it's caused so much upset, I felt—I had to see you and explain. And apologize.' Red-faced, he lapsed into an awkward silence.

Cassie stared at him. On the one hand she wanted to believe him; on the other, it could so easily be Guy's clever way of winning back her confidence. Judging by his past record, she wouldn't put that past him.

'Well,' she said, turning away so that he wouldn't see her uncertainty, 'it was kind of you to take the trouble. But I still think that this is between Guy and me.'

'He's very fond of you, you know.'

'Is he?' Her tone was cynical.

'Yes. He really went for me when I said what I did, and I've never known him to do that before.'

'I'm sure I'm very flattered. Perhaps you'll thank him for me when you see him.' Cassie wasn't going to give way; to show any weakness now would be courting trouble. Charles sighed.

'All right, I suppose there's no more that I can say.

But I hope you'll understand that Guy was in no way to blame.'

Cassie turned to face him. 'I'll think it over, Mr Martin. But I don't think it's going to make much difference.'

Charles shrugged. 'Then I'll say goodbye, and bon voyage.'

'Thank you.' She waited until the door closed after him, then turned back to her suitcases.

She was confused and more than a little stunned by what Charles had said. In so many ways it rang true; after all, she had overheard only his side of the conversation, and for all she knew Guy might as well have been defending her as joining in the joke. But there was one factor that didn't fit, and one that Charles probably didn't know about. Guy had already been seen with another girl—in fact as far as Cassie knew he was entertaining her to dinner in the hotel right now. Cassie had seen them coming into the lobby, the girl—a pretty but rather dumb-looking blonde—hanging on to his arm and gazing into his eyes. Already he seemed to have reverted to his favourite pastime, and the thought of it made Cassie feel sick with—what? Anger? Jealousy? She didn't want to answer that question. But whatever the case, certainly Guy seemed to have forgotten her all too easily. And that was something that didn't figure in Charles Martin's attempt to explain everything.

Suddenly furious, Cassie started thrusting belongings into her case, throwing them in anyhow as if she could vent her fury on them. Then the phone rang.

She snatched up the receiver and snapped, 'Yes?'

'Chérie?' Anna's voice crackled down the line. 'You sound like the thunderstorm!'

'Anna—oh, I'm terribly sorry, I had no idea it would be you.'

'Well it is, and I am most put out. You promised to come back and see me, and you have not. And now Alan tells me you are flying home tomorrow! You cannot get away from your friends so easily; you shall come now to my suite for a farewell drink, or I shall be very angry indeed!' There was laughter in her voice and, as always, it had a cheering effect on Cassie.

'Anna, I'm sorry,' she said again. 'Of course I'll come at once.'

'If not sooner.' And with another laugh Anna put the receiver down.

Cassie hurried to the Frenchwoman's suite, where she found an enormous cocktail—one of Anna's more exotic favourites—waiting for her.

'So,' Anna said, taking a sip from her own glass, 'we are to lose you, *hein?* A great pity—you are wasted in Australia!'

Cassie smiled. 'I'll be glad to get home, Anna.'

'Oh? A sudden change, I think—are you not happy here?'

'Not happy, no.'

The actress stared hard at her, then, 'Ye-es...it is in your eyes, and it has nothing to do with your work. It is Guy, is it not?'

Cassie's quick denial was *too* quick; she knew even as she spoke that she had given herself away. And Anna knew it too.

'Do not play games, *chérie*. You cannot hide what you are feeling, and anyway I know all about it.'

'You *know?*'

Anna nodded. 'Guy has told me. He is very unhappy.'

'Is he?' Cassie's voice was bitter. 'I doubt it.'

179

'You are in no position to judge. He told me what happened between you and that now you will not let him explain the truth to you.'

'There wouldn't be any point,' Cassie said sadly. 'Even if he did explain, I don't think I could believe him.'

'Why not? Because of his bad reputation? Ah, it is like the boy who cried wolf—when the wolf really came no one believed his warning, and so the sheep were all gobbled up. I cannot blame you for that. But I have known Guy a long time, and I know when he is lying and when he is sincere. *Chérie,* I think you have broken his heart.'

Cassie's own heart seemed to skip a beat, then start again painfully fast. *Guy—heartbroken . . . ?*

'You are important to him, *chérie,*' Anna added quietly. 'More important, I think, than anything has been for a very long time.'

Cassie wanted to believe her; she wanted to let down the barriers of anger and resentment that had built up since the visit to Sussex. But it would be like clutching at straws . . . Miserably she shook her head. 'That's very sweet of you, Anna, and it may even be true, I don't know. But if it *is* true, how long would it last before he got as bored with me as he's got with all the others?' And as the Frenchwoman started to speak again she interrupted her. 'No, please don't say anything. I really appreciate what you're trying to do for me. I have fallen in love with Guy, and I still do love him despite everything that's happened. But I can't let it go on. He might feel something for me now, but it wouldn't last. In the long run I could never be anything more than one girlfriend among dozens, and I—I don't think I could bear that. It would hurt too much,'

'More than it hurts now?' Anna asked.

Cassie thought about that, then nodded. 'Yes. Much more. If I break off now and go back to Australia, I'll get over him eventually. I've got a horrible feeling that it will take a long time, but it can't last forever.'

Tears were beginning to fall, but she made no attempt to stop them; with Anna, somehow, it didn't matter—she understood. She looked up, her vision suddenly blurred. 'And one thing's certain, Anna. I won't ever make the mistake of falling in love with a famous man again. I'm not cut out for it; it's too harsh. I just can't stand up to the competition.'

14

The flight to Sydney was due to leave early in the morning, and by five-thirty Cassie was up, after a near sleepless night. She had had a succession of unhappy dreams about Guy and finally had forced herself to stay awake for the rest of the night, too afraid of the effect the dreams were having on her to risk any more.

She was thankful that she had left her packing until the last moment, because, as she had expected, there were matters preying on her mind which she did not want to dwell on, and having to concentrate on sorting out her clothes was a relief. But as she folded dresses and jeans and blouses and put them away, she still found that the image of Guy's face was slipping back into her inner vision. She could see him in her mind's eye as clearly as if he were standing in the room with her—the black hair framing the expressive, bony face, the vivid grey eyes watching her, the lightly-built frame leaning up against the car in which he had taken her to Sussex... And then there were images of his home—the tangled garden, tea in the sitting-room, the warm bedroom...

Cassie bit her lip savagely. She mustn't think about him. But she couldn't help it; those images were firmly implanted and she felt that they would be with her wherever she went. Back home in Australia, thousands of miles away, Guy Carver was going to haunt her.

The phone rang, and she picked it up. It was Alan, sounding sleepy.

'Cass? How's your packing going? We've got to leave soon.'

'Fine—I'm nearly ready.' There was a catch in her voice but Alan didn't comment on it. No doubt once they were on the plane he would start asking questions. But they would be easier to answer when she was thousands of feet above the English landscape and winging home. Would they fly over Sussex, she wondered . . . ?

'Good girl. As soon as I've finished here I'll come to your room, all right? I've arranged for a car.'

'All right. See you in a little while.' She hung up and stared at the hotel room, taking it all in properly for the last time. So many memories in such a short time. The scene before her blurred, and she sat down on the bed, telling herself fiercely that this lapse was nothing; she always felt peculiar when she was leaving a place, though God knew she ought to be used to it by now. And deep down a little voice was saying over and over, *Liar!*

If only she could go back to Sydney and never have to see London again it would be so much easier. But even if the film was never completed, she would have to return for the court case against Van Hamer and Andrew Symes. And then—

Someone knocked, and she thought that Alan had been quicker than she had anticipated. 'Come in.'

She heard the door open and close, but didn't turn round. Forcing cheerfulness into her voice she said, 'You've been quick! I'm not finished here yet, but I'd love a cup of coffee.'

'I'll ring room service for you,' said Guy's voice.

Cassie spun round. He was standing in the room,

dressed in a light shirt and jeans and looking as though he hadn't slept all night. There were dark shadows under his eyes, and the crisp black hair, normally so tidy, was tousled.

'Oh God . . .' said Cassie.

He stepped forward and immediately, instinctively, she backed a pace. 'Guy, please—go away.' The catch was back in her voice; it was near breaking point, and she knew as she looked at him that she couldn't hold out for long against the wave of emotion that threatened to swamp her. If he would only get out of the room she would be all right. But he didn't.

'No,' he said firmly, 'I've got something to say, and I'm going to say it. And you're going to listen.'

She wanted to run to him, throw her arms round him. Fighting the urge, she looked away. 'No!' she said savagely. 'Please—I don't want to hear it. I just want you to leave me alone!'

Guy said, 'Do you?' And Cassie couldn't control herself any longer. Covering her face with both hands she said brokenly, 'Guy, haven't you done enough? I don't want to talk to you. I don't even want to look at you, because . . .' She couldn't finish the sentence. 'It isn't fair,' she whispered, 'please, don't do this to me. Just go, and let me get away without any of this . . .'

'That's just what I'm not going to do.' She heard him move towards her and jumped when suddenly his hands took hold of her arms. She tried to pull away but he held on.

'Sit down, Cassie, and *listen*,' he told her. 'It's vitally important—you've got to hear me out.'

He was propelling her towards the bed, and she subsided on to it. When she looked up he was crouching beside her and their faces were on a level. His eyes were painfully intense.

'I've been talking to Anna,' he said, 'and she's told me about your conversation with her last night. You mustn't be angry with her—she's done us both a great favour. If it hadn't been for her, you'd be making a big mistake right now.'

'Mistake?' Cassie demanded, her voice trembling as fresh tears pricked her eyes. 'How can you say any thing like that? After what—'

Guy didn't try to stop her anger with words. Instead he leaned forward and before Cassie could stop him his lips had found hers and he was kissing her forcibly, his hand touching her face with that tenderness she remembered so well. When he finally released her she was shaking like a leaf, and as soon as she could she turned her head away, saying bitterly, 'Did you do that to the girl you were with last night?'

'No, I did not.' He pulled her round to face him again. 'I took her to dinner because I was trying to forget about you. I thought I could find a substitute. I was very, very wrong, and when I put her into a taxi and sent her home straight after the meal, she wasn't very pleased. That's sure to be in the gossip columns before long, and if they ask me why I did it, I'll tell them it was because she wasn't the girl I love.'

Cassie stared at him. She tried to tell herself he was lying, playing with her—she had to believe that, or all her defences would be worthless.

'You've got a choice to make,' Guy told her, 'and you've got to make it right now. Either you get on that flight to Sydney and you go home, or—' He paused, looking embarrassed, then suddenly he said, 'Oh hell, I'm useless at this. I can propose marriage to women in front of a camera and I can make it sound totally convincing. But when it comes to the real thing, I don't know where to begin, what to do... Cassie, your other choice is to wait until the register office opens, come with me and get a special licence, and—if they can fit us in, we'll be married by lunchtime.'

Cassie continued to stare at him as the full implication of what he had said hit her. For a moment she thought that this was some kind of a joke, that he was still playing with her. But he couldn't be, not about something like this... She began to feel as though the bed beneath her was spinning and about to throw her off into black space.

Guy said, 'Cassie, I'm deadly serious.' He took both her hands. 'I can't bear to see you like this. Charles told me that he explained that dreadful mistake to you, and when you still wouldn't listen to him, I—I knew I had to do something drastic. I was going to wait, give you time, because I didn't think you'd believe me if I said that I wanted you for my wife. But I can't wait; not when you're booked to fly home. I love you, Cass, like I've never loved anyone, and I want you.' He smiled slightly, hopefully. 'I'm a selfish man, and a very impatient one. If you say no, I won't let go, because I want you and nothing's going to stop me getting my own way. If you refuse, I'll—well, I'll bulldoze you into accepting me if it's the only way. If you won't say yes now, then I won't give up. I'll follow you to Australia if I have to. Wouldn't it save us both a lot of time and trouble if you agreed right this minute...?

He was half-laughing with embarrassment and nervousness, and in that moment Cassie realized that he could not possibly be playing with her. She had been wrong, terribly wrong about him, and both Anna and

Charles had seen it long before she had. All this pain and anguish had been for nothing; she felt as if she were caught up in a dream as all the images that had haunted her came flooding back. But this time the dream wasn't going to break and turn to nothing.

Guy leaned forward again suddenly, and his head bowed on her knees. 'Cassie...' he said.

Trembling, her hand reached out and touched his black hair. It felt like rough silk under her fingers, and she stroked it.

'Oh God, Guy,' she whispered, *I love you.'*

He raised his head, and when their eyes met, his were half-wild with a passion and a joy that she had never seen in them before. 'Then—you'll say yes?' he asked her.

'Yes. Yes, yes, yes.' Even as she spoke, Cassie's voice broke into a mixture of laughter and tears, and Guy's arms slipped round her, pulling her hard against him and holding her until she thought she would break in his embrace. She reached her face towards his and they kissed for a second time. Her heart could have burst with happiness at that moment. Words were beyond her, and she could only hold on to Guy and try to express what she was feeling with her lips and with her body.

Alan had never been the most tactful of people, and he burst into the room without knocking, to find them sitting on the bed, Guy's arms tightly around Cassie and her head on his shoulder as he clasped her. Alan stopped, his eyebrows shooting up, and said loudly, 'I'm sorry to break up the farewell party, but—'

They looked up, and it was as if they didn't see him. Then Cassie shook her head dazedly. 'Alan...'

He pointed to his watch. 'We've got to check in at Heathrow in an hour and—good grief, woman, you haven't even finished packing!'

For a moment Cassie and Guy looked at each other again. Then, as one, they began to laugh.

'What's so funny?' Alan demanded agitatedly. 'If we don't get there on time, we'll miss the flight!'

Guy touched Cassie's face tenderly. 'Go on,' he said, 'you tell him.'

Cassie faced Alan, and swallowed. Disentangling herself a little from Guy's hold, she said, 'Alan, I've got something to tell you—another bolt out of the blue I'm afraid.'

Alan looked blank, and she went on, 'You'll have to tell them that they'll be one short on the Sydney flight. You see—' She looked into Guy's grey eyes again, and the laughter in them matched her own joy. 'I've got an appointment today. A very special appointment. And nothing on this earth is going to stop me from keeping it!'